PRINCESS
IN THE OUTBACK

PRINCESS IN THE OUTBACK

BY
BARBARA HANNAY

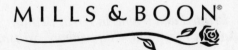

MILLS & BOON®

First published in Great Britain 2004
Large Print edition 2004
Harlequin Mills & Boon Limited,
Eton House, 18-24 Paradise Road,
Richmond, Surrey TW9 1SR

© Barbara Hannay 2004

ISBN 0 263 18096 4

Set in Times Roman 16½ on 18½ pt.
16-0804-45813

Printed and bound in Great Britain
by Antony Rowe Ltd, Chippenham, Wiltshire

CHAPTER ONE

THE first pale fingers of wintry dawn crept through the hospital as Isabella left the ward. Time to get home to a long, hot bath and a steaming cup of ginger tea. Then sleep.

Cheered by thoughts of comfort and warmth, she pulled her thick woollen cape over her shoulders, wrapped a long red scarf about her head, and prepared to face the icy blast outside.

'Your Highness?'

She turned, surprised to see her personal physician, Dr Christos Tenni, hurrying towards her down the chilly corridor.

'You look very tired,' he said when he reached her. 'You're working too hard.'

'Nonsense, Christos. You know I thrive on this work. It makes up for all the razzmatazz.'

But, despite her blithe response, Isabella felt a stab of alarm. Her good friend looked worried, almost frightened. It was rather unnerving to see one of Amoria's most level-headed and respected physicians throwing hasty glances over his shoulder, as if he needed to ensure that he wasn't overheard.

'You've been here all night,' he insisted. 'You must be exhausted. Please have something to eat and drink now, before you leave.'

'All right. Coffee would be lovely,' she said, lowering her voice to match his furtive manner.

He escorted her across the highly waxed corridor into his office and closed the door. She frowned when he pulled a bolt across, and her frown deepened when she saw that his desk had been set with a silver coffee pot, two fine gilt-edged porcelain cups and saucers and a platter covered by an engraved silver dome. It was most unusual for the hospital staff to worry about royal protocol at such an early hour.

Trying to stay calm, she unwound her scarf and massaged the stiffness in her neck, a legacy from the night she'd spent on a hard hospital chair while she held the hand of a lonely dying man.

The doctor poured her coffee, and as he handed her the cup he glanced again towards the door.

'Christos, what's the matter? You seem very on edge.'

He didn't answer until he'd walked around to the other side of the desk and was seated. Then he seemed to take great care to compose his features into a calm and benign mask, and Isabella couldn't help fearing that this was how he looked when he was about to tell his patients bad news.

'My dear Princess Isabella,' he said slowly, leaning towards her with his strong, neat hands clasped on the desk in front of him, his voice barely above a whisper. 'You are in grave danger.'

Her hands shook and her coffee cup rattled against its saucer as she set it back on his desk. 'What—what kind of danger?'

He took a long, deep breath, and the pained expression on his face suggested he was hating this moment. 'I'm very sorry to be the bearer of this news, but it has come to my notice that your fiancé, the Count of Montez, means to harm you.'

'For heaven's sake!' Isabella gaped at him. 'You must be wrong. How could Radik want to hurt me? It's ridiculous. He—he loves me.'

Dr. Tenni cleared his throat. 'Isabella—your Highness—'

'Please, Christos, forget the formalities. We're friends.'

'Isabella, you've known me all your life.'

'Yes, but I can't believe this.'

'If I told you something about your health—even that you had a life-threatening illness—you would trust me, wouldn't you? You'd believe me?'

'Yes…'

'Then please believe me when I tell you that you're fit and in wonderful health, but you won't live your life to its full span if you marry Count Radik.'

'*No!*'

'I'm afraid it's the truth.'

'But why? What on earth has happened?'

The doctor rose and came around his desk to stand beside Isabella's chair. He rested his hand gently on her shoulder. 'When I was in Geneva last week I overheard a conversation between the Count of Montez and a woman.'

She couldn't suppress an involuntary shudder. 'Marina Prideaux?'

'You know about her?'

Oh, God. This was awful. Just last week she'd walked into Radik's rooms and quite inadvertently seen a letter he'd been writing to a woman he'd called *My Darling Poodle*. When she'd mentioned it Radik had been furious, unjustifiably so.

She was quite sure he'd been writing to Marina Prideaux... *Darling Poodle.*

'I don't know much, except that she was Radik's girlfriend some time ago, but I must admit—' She drew a sharp breath. 'So he's still seeing her?'

'Yes, but I'm afraid that's not all.'

A cold wave of nausea rose from her stomach to her throat. 'Just tell me the worst,

Christos. You're—you're frightening me terribly.'

He squeezed her hand. 'I'm so sorry, Isabella. The Count of Montez seems to view your wedding as a merger rather than a true marriage.'

'A merger?'

'I know he wouldn't be the first man to marry into royalty to gain access to money and wealthy estates, but this time there is more at stake. I heard him reassuring the Prideaux woman that he still loves *her* and that she just has to be patient. Within six weeks of your marriage he plans for you to have an unfortunate accident—most probably a car crash, because everyone knows how treacherous the Alpine roads in Amoria can be.'

'Oh, God!'

Had Christos gone mad? How could Radik want to kill her?

'He knows that after your—ah—demise he will still be able to retain his entitlement to a handsome percentage of your worldly goods,' Christos added.

'It can't be true,' she whispered. But even as the denial left her lips she felt a ghastly suspicion that Christos Tenni was correct. She stared back into the doctor's worried face and her stomach took a sickening plunge. His preposterous claims had touched a raw nerve, exposing things about her fiancé she'd been working hard to overlook.

Radik, the Count of Montez, was as handsome and glamorous a suitor as any European princess could hope for. He'd waltzed into her life eight months ago and she'd been swept away by his dashing charm.

Oh, he'd flirted prettily with her, flattered her and brought her little presents. He'd escorted her to glittering social occasions— kissed her.

She knew that under her father's strict governance she'd been overly protected. Compared with most young women she was naïve about the ways of men and romance, but, on the whole, the experience of being engaged had been very pleasant.

Until recently…

Apart from the incident with the letter, lately she'd sensed the cold flicker of something like menace in her fiancé's handsome dark eyes. It lurked behind his smooth smile and caused her sleepless nights.

And there was his mounting obsession with money…

She drew in a sharp breath. If she was completely honest with herself, she had to admit that there had been rather too many disappointments. Radik had shown little interest in her charity work. She'd tried to suppress her growing feeling that something wasn't quite right about the royal engagement. There'd never been talk of love.

God knew, she'd tried to ignore her qualms. The very thought of speaking to her father about breaking off a royal engagement filled her with dread. It was like trying to hold back a tidal wave single-handed.

But if it was a choice between that and her death?

She jumped out of the chair. 'What can I do? The wedding's next week. The newspapers are full of it.'

Every detail had been followed closely by the Amorian public: the wedding gown made by a Parisian couturier; the wedding cakes baked in San Sebastián from a traditional royal recipe and transported to Madrid to be iced; the presents that had been flooding in from all over the world.

Gifts of jewellery, clocks, decanters, candlesticks, pieces of silver, antique furniture and tapestries had all been placed on display in the Valdenza Palace in aid of charity.

A magazine had even leaked details of the wardrobe Radik insisted she needed for their glamorous honeymoon—three morning ensembles, five afternoon dresses, six evening gowns, two coats.

'I *can't* ask my father to call off the wedding at this late stage.'

'I'm afraid you must,' Christos said gravely.

'But Father will have apoplexy. He urged me to marry Radik. His advisers all supported it. They think he's wonderful. Perfect.'

'I'll admit it won't be easy. His Majesty's friends have always been strong supporters of the Montez family and they'll be loath to admit a mistake now.' Christos's eyes gleamed damply as he looked at Isabella. 'But think of what's at stake, my dear.'

She felt a surge of panic, as if she were running through a maze, turning corner after corner only to find her way blocked at every turn. 'I'm not even sure that Father would listen to me. He'll probably think I'm just having pre-wedding nerves.'

Oh, mercy! Isabella pressed a hand to her hammering heart.

She began to pace the office, folding her arms across her stomach. She bowed her head as she tried to think through the horrified tumble of her thoughts.

'Christos, what should I do?'

'If your mother was still alive—' the doctor began, and then paused and cleared his throat. 'You've always had unerring instincts. It's what makes you so wonderfully sensitive with the patients here. You should trust those inner promptings now.'

Yes, she should. The more she thought, the more she was sure of that. 'Whatever happens, I mustn't marry him,' she said, and with the announcement she felt a flood of relief. Despite the shock of learning that her life was in danger, she was suddenly free of a shadowy but worrying burden.

At least she could be grateful that she'd never given in to Radik's attempts to seduce her. How awful to have discovered too late that she'd squandered her love on an A-grade cad.

But deciding to call the wedding off was one thing. Finding the courage to do so, marshalling the nerve to speak to her father, would be a very different matter.

'Christos, will you come with me when I speak to my father?'

'Of course.'

'I'm afraid he won't be back from New York for another two days.'

'That's a pity.' He sighed and looked thoughtful. 'I don't think it would be wise to discuss this over the telephone.'

'No, but I'll make sure we can see him the very minute he returns.'

'Very well. That will have to do.' Christos hugged her. 'In the meantime, be very careful, my dear. I don't wish to alarm you any more than I have, but I think I'm being watched.'

CHAPTER TWO

A THUNDEROUS racket woke Jack.

It penetrated his dreams and sent his heart racing. Adrenalin did the rest, priming his body into action before he was properly awake. In one seamless motion he yanked his sleeping bag aside and leapt from the bed.

Rain as hard as bullets pelted against the hut's corrugated iron roof, and over its drumming he heard a thumping and crashing sound—something or some*body* trying to break his door down.

With no moonlight or starlight to guide him, he stumbled towards the door and stubbed his toe on the metal-framed bed. He let fly with a loud curse and was still cursing as he wrenched the door open.

Sharp, stinging rain needled his face, and a second later a very wet body pitched past him into the hut.

17

'What the—?'

He couldn't see a darned thing, but someone was shivering and gasping in the dark beside him.

'What do you want?' he shouted as he stepped back and dragged the door shut against the driving rain. 'What are you doing out here?'

The only answer was his intruder's breathless panting.

What the blazes was going on? His instructions had been clear. He'd insisted on no interruptions. This week was his time off. A week of solitude and sanctuary in the remote bush at Pelican's End. Away from the office, the phone, the fax and e-mail. Out of contact in the Outback.

Apparently not.

'Sit there. I'll find a light.' Reaching out into the darkness, he shoved the shivering figure down onto the bed then groped his way towards the rough-timbered kitchen bench. After a few blind miss-tries, his fingers closed over a box of matches. He struck a light, lifted the lantern glass and held the match to the wick.

Soft light leapt around the small interior of the tiny one-roomed hut, bringing to life the ripple iron walls, the simple rustic furnishings and the crude stone floor. Holding the lantern at head height, Jack turned to inspect the intruder. And was met by an ear-splitting scream.

Bloody hell! A woman. He nearly dropped the lamp.

Dumping the lantern back on the bench, he snatched his jeans from the floor and rammed the zip into place so fast he almost did himself serious injury.

'Stop screaming! I'm not going to hurt you.'

She stopped the noise but remained huddled on his bed, wet and whimpering, looking up at him with dark, frightened eyes, huge in her pale, oval face.

What the heck was a woman doing out here, roaming around this isolated neck of the Outback in the middle of a stormy night?

She was young, at a guess in her mid-twenties. And very wet. Drowned-rat wet. Her black hair fell to her shoulders in a wild and sodden tangle and the rain had made her white shirt transparent. Her drenched denim skirt clung to her slim, pale thighs, revealing slender mud-splattered legs and a grazed knee. Her trainers were soaked and covered with slippery mud.

Shakily she rose to her feet, looked down at the bedding and muttered something in a foreign language that he couldn't make out.

'My French is rusty,' he said. 'Can you speak English?'

She frowned and pressed her fingers to her right temple, but this time when she spoke the words sounded like Spanish.

Terrific. Not only did he have a hysterical stranger invading his precious retreat and ruining his sleep, but he had communication problems as well. 'English,' he demanded. 'Hello? Goodnight? How are you? Can you speak English?'

'Yes,' she said at last. 'Yes, of course I can speak English.'

Jack's eyebrows lifted. She spoke English all right—with a cultured intonation hinting of Oxbridge.

'Good. Now, listen, I'm not going to hurt you.'

She nodded. 'Thank you.' Then she looked around her. 'Do you have a telephone?'

'Telephone? You've got to be joking. I don't even have electricity out here.'

'I see.' She looked down at the bed and pointed to the damp patch she'd made. 'I'm being a nuisance. Look, I've made your bed wet.'

'I'll get you a towel,' he said, dredging up a reluctant gallantry.

There were a couple of thick towels in his pack on the floor and he dragged one out. As he offered it to her he realised she was still shivering. 'You're soaked through.'

With two fingers she pulled the sodden sleeve of her shirt away from her arm. Rivulets of muddy water ran down her elbow and dripped onto the floor. She stared at the puddle that had formed at her feet.

'What happened?' he asked.

'I must have taken a wrong turn off the highway and I think I crashed my car into a river.'

'You *think* you crashed it?'

She looked up at him and her dark eyes clouded with bewilderment. 'I—I don't really know for sure—the water was coming up so fast. One moment I was on a track and next— I—there was water everywhere.'

With a surge of dismay he saw the colour leaching from her face. Then her hand wavered up to cover her mouth as a soft moan escaped. She swayed and her eyelids drooped closed.

'Hey, steady, there.' Taking her by the shoulders, he lowered her back to the bed. 'Don't start fainting on me.' He rolled his swag and bedding out of the way, exposing the bare mattress. 'Get your head down. A little damp won't hurt this old mattress.'

Gingerly, she stretched out on the bare ticking mattress, and he frowned as he saw how very pale her cheeks and lips remained. 'Are you hurt?'

'I think I must have banged my head.'

Bringing the lantern closer, he set it on a stool beside the bed. Then he gently patted her hair with the towel, searching as he did so for signs of injury. Once or twice she winced, but there was no blood and he couldn't find a wound.

'Was there anyone else with you?'

'No.'

That was a relief. At least he didn't have to go charging off into the stormy darkness to test his heroism in a flooded creek.

She lay very quietly with her eyes closed as he lifted the heavy dark hair from her shoulders and wound the towel around it, squeezing out the moisture. He tried not to look at her wet blouse, but he could see straight through it to her white lacy bra and the rise and fall of her breasts, exaggerated by her frightened breathing.

'What's your name?' he asked.

Her eyes flashed wide open and he saw how very dark her irises were—really, really dark, almost black—and fringed with thick black lashes. She stared at him without speaking, and after a prolonged moment of silence she opened her mouth to say something, but then she turned away and closed her eyes again.

Jack frowned and abandoned the questions. There wasn't much point in grilling her anyhow. She was a foreign tourist stuck in this isolated drover's shack in the middle of the Outback at the start of the wet season and her car was lying in the bottom of a flooded creek. Where she came from wasn't half as relevant as how she was going to get out again, and the prospects weren't too good.

But, for now, she needed to get out of these wet clothes.

'We'll have to get you dry.' He turned and dragged a long-sleeved shirt from his pack. It was a heavy denim number, and should be enough to keep her warm. 'You can put this on.'

She didn't answer.

Turning back to her, he frowned. 'Can you manage by yourself?'

She was very still as she lay on the bed with her eyes closed. Her cheeks were too pale. Had she fainted?

'Hello?' he said, tapping her shoulder.

She moaned softly, in what sounded like Spanish, but he could hardly hear her above the thunder of the rain on the roof.

'Hey, Carmen,' he called, grabbing for the first Spanish name that jumped into his head. 'Don't go to sleep till you've got dry clothes on.'

Still she didn't answer.

Hell, she was out to it. Could she have concussion? Jack knew it was selfish, but he felt a stirring of resentment. A mercy dash to a hospital would completely wreck his plans. Besides, it could be impossible. From what she'd told him they were probably cut off by the creek.

One thing was certain: he couldn't leave her lying in those wet things. He wiped a hand over his brow. It wasn't as if he'd never removed a woman's clothing before, but in the past he'd had the advantage of the other party's consent and open-hearted co-operation.

Taking a deep breath, he gingerly unbuttoned her blouse and peeled the wet cotton away from her, lifting her shoulders as he slipped her arms out of the sleeves.

It was impossible not to notice how neat and pretty she was. Her skin had the kind of soft, white flawless perfection that was impossible for a sun-drenched Australian girl. Her collarbones were exquisitely symmetrical, her shoulders smooth and round. His hands shook slightly as he unsnapped her wet bra and removed it to reveal her pale breasts, small and round and tipped with delicate rosy peaks. Oh, God. Swiftly he covered her with the towel and began to rub her arms vigorously.

The rough movements seemed to rouse her. Her eyes opened and she cried out in alarm when she saw him bending over her.

'*Au secours!* Don't touch me!'

He dropped the towel to cover her. 'Calm down. I was trying to get you dry. You passed out.'

Obviously she didn't believe him. She jerked quickly into a sitting position and the towel slipped. Her eyes were huge and terrified as she glared at him.

Jack grabbed the towel from her lap and shoved it at her. 'You have to get dry,' he growled. 'Do it yourself. Just get the rest of those wet things off and put this shirt on.' He scowled at her. 'And stop looking at me like I'm going to eat you. I've had my dinner.'

'Would you please turn away?' she asked, clutching the towel to her chest.

'Naturally,' he drawled, sending her a gritted-teeth smile. 'And I'll boil the billy for some tea.'

'Boil the billy?'

'Boil water *in* a billy and make a cup of tea.' He spoke with exaggerated patience, then very deliberately turned his back on her and made a business of fiddling with a small gas ring. 'You let me know when you're done.'

As he filled the kettle with water from the tank in the corner, and rummaged for an extra mug, the downpour on the roof continued. If it kept raining at this rate the creek would flood its banks. He wished he'd paid more attention to the weather forecasts, but he'd been too keen to grab the chance to get away. He would have come to the hut whatever the predictions had been.

Of course if he'd been here on his own he wouldn't have cared two hoots about the rain. The hut was on high ground, and if the creeks cut him off all the better. No one could get near him. He'd be assured of the solitude he craved.

But with this woman here now he needed the rain to stop. He needed to get her out.

He was aware of her hesitant movements behind him as she removed her shoes and the rest of her clothing. And he was annoyed when his mind kept straying to thoughts of how the bottom half of this stranger would be as lovely as her top half.

'You'll have to have your tea black. There's no milk,' he called over his shoulder. 'Do you take sugar?'

'A teaspoon of sugar, thank you.'

As he stirred the sugar and broke open a packet of oatmeal biscuits a flapping movement in his peripheral vision caught his attention. He saw that she'd finished the drying process and had put his shirt on. It was huge on her, hanging down to her knees, with the sleeves extending way beyond her hands. She was rolling them back with small neat movements.

'It's just your size,' he said. 'A perfect fit.'

In the lamplight he saw her mouth twitch into a tiny *almost* smile. 'It's very good of you to lend me your shirt.'

'Do you think you'll be warm enough?'

'Yes. I am very comfortable now.'

He walked closer, caught her chin between a forefinger and thumb and peered into her eyes. Both pupils seemed evenly dilated. 'How many fingers?' he asked, holding two in front of her.

'Two.'

'Terrific.' He handed her a mug and pointed to the three-legged stool beside the bed. 'Take a seat and drink this.'

'Thank you.' As she took the mug she said, 'You are very kind.'

Jack didn't agree. He wasn't being kind. He'd had no choice. 'I could hardly have left you out in the storm.'

Using an upturned fuel drum for a seat, he sat, and they sipped their tea in the gentle lamplight while thunder rolled and rain crashed on the roof and against the walls.

'How are you feeling now?' he asked. 'You had me worried when you blacked out before.'

'My head hurts a little, but I feel much better, thank you.' She touched the side of her head and lifted her damp wild hair back from her face. He couldn't help noting that the bone structure of her face and hands was exquisite. Was there such a thing as a high-class gypsy? That was how she looked to him. Carmen with class.

'Do you realise how lucky you were to find this place in the dark?'

She shivered. 'The lightning showed me the way. I was so scared, but it lit up the bush and I could see the track because it was shiny with wet mud. So I followed it up from the creek and—and I bumped into your hut.'

He had to admit she'd been rather brave to set off through the bush in the storm. 'What are you doing way out here anyway?' he asked. 'Where were you heading?'

She looked worried again, as if she needed to consider the best way to answer his simple question.

For a nanosecond Jack wondered if she was on the run, then dismissed the notion as fanciful in the extreme. Just the same, he knew in his bones that she had a secret or two. But, hell, didn't everyone?

'I was driving down from Darwin. I'm on my way to visit friends,' she said, and suddenly she sat a little straighter and leaned forward, extending her hand towards him. 'My name is Isabella Martineau.' She sounded very formal, even a little haughty.

'Isabella,' he repeated, returning her handshake. 'Hi.'

He guessed a fancy name like Isabella suited her, but for some odd reason he preferred to think of her as Carmen. 'I'm Jack,' he said quickly. 'Jack...' He paused, suddenly unwilling to give his family name. His parents were so well known that even foreigners seemed to have heard of them. If he couldn't have solitude, at least he could have anonymity. 'So, what are you doing in the Northern Territory?' he asked to cover his evasion. 'Are you a backpacker?'

'No.' Her reply was abrupt, as if she was as reluctant to disclose personal details as he was. She took another deep gulp of tea, looked down at something on her leg and screamed again.

'What is it this time? What's the matter?'

Her mouth trembled as she pointed. 'Are th-they l-leeches?'

He studied her leg. Sure enough, two slick black leeches were clinging to her ankle. One of them had grown quite shiny and swollen with her blood. 'Yeah, they're leeches all right.'

'Oh, God.'

'You must have picked them up down near the creek. Nasty little bloodsuckers, aren't they?'

She shuddered and looked ill. 'Please, can you pull them off?'

'I can, but it'll make you bleed too much. Hang on, I've got a better way.'

Grabbing the box of matches from the bench, he returned quickly to crouch beside her, but she jerked her legs away from him. The dark wariness in her eyes told him she still didn't trust him.

'Don't panic. I'm not into torturing women for kicks, but some carefully applied heat will make these little mongrels let go.'

She drew a deep, shuddering breath, as if gathering strength for an ordeal. 'Thank you,' she whispered, and gingerly moved her leg closer to him once more.

With one knee bent, Jack lifted her foot and rested it on his thigh, then lit a match. She leaned forward, her dark head close to his, her eyes fearful as he slipped one hand behind her shapely calf and took hold of her, keeping her leg steady as he lowered the match. 'Hold still now,' he murmured. 'I just want to get a little heat close to him.'

He could feel tension vibrating through her as he guided the small flame closer. Hell, there was tension in him, too, but it wasn't fear. It was too long since he'd been this close to a beautiful woman.

The instant the leeches sensed the heat they released their grip and it was a simple matter to remove them. They left pinpricks of bright blood on her skin.

'Thank you,' she murmured fervently as he blew out the match. Her dark eyes were very close to his and he realised he was still holding her leg.

'Let's check your other leg and make sure you don't have any more,' he said abruptly as he took his hand away.

She lowered one foot and lifted the other. Her foot fitted neatly against the curve of his thigh. Too neatly. He quickly scanned her leg. No sign of leeches, but her skin was smooth, her ankle trim, her foot daintily arched. Yeah, the bottom half of her seemed to be every bit as pleasing to the eye as the top half.

Annoyed to catch himself thinking like that, he lifted her leg and swung his thigh well clear of her, then jumped to his feet. 'I think we've got rid of the lot. Would you like some more tea?'

She shook her head and winced, as if the movement hurt her.

'You need to rest. There's nothing more we can do tonight.'

Scanning the room, her dark eyes grew wide and worried again. 'There's only one little bed.'

He considered teasing her, suggesting that they would have to share it, but figured she'd had enough nasty surprises for one night. 'I know this isn't a palace, but there's a fold-out stretcher over in the corner.' He risked a grin. 'There's plenty of room for the two of us.'

The savoury aroma of frying sausages woke Isabella. Her first feeling was surprise that she'd slept so well. The constant drumming of rain on the roof must have worked on her like a non-stop lullaby.

But then came an onslaught of memories, slamming into her like physical blows, bringing again the ghastly shock of Christos Tenni's death. The poor man had been killed by a hit-and-run driver as he was crossing the road in front of the hospital.

She'd flown into a horrified panic. Her father was still away and she'd felt so suddenly ill and alone and vulnerable that her only thought had been to escape from Radik—from Amoria.

But when she'd reached the other side of the world she'd driven headlong from one danger straight into the jaws of another—the terrifying flood of creek water, the struggle to escape through the current. And now she'd lost everything—her passport, clothes and all her money.

And where on earth was she?

Her eyes adjusted to the gloomy interior of Jack's hut, and she tried to calm herself by taking in details of her surroundings.

It was still raining outside. There was only one small square of foggy window pane, which let in a faint stream of murky light to reveal a very humble hut. Above her a rusty iron roof sagged and the rain dripped through a hole in the corner into a blue plastic bucket. Nails had been driven into the walls to hang old horseshoes, a battered hat, rolls of wire and ancient cooking utensils.

She thought of her bedroom in the palace, where her maid Toinette tiptoed across thick carpet to draw back whisper-quiet velvet drapes from floor-to-ceiling double-glazed windows.

Here the floor was made of stone and needed a good sweeping and—oh, no—in the corner there were huge, thick spider webs! *Help!* Had spiders crawled over her during the night? Had their ghastly hairy legs touched her? Could they bite?

She sat bolt upright and spun around, looking for Jack.

He was over by the kitchen bench, standing with his back to her, slowly turning sausages in a pan on a gas ring.

He didn't seem too bothered about spiders.

Her fear subsided as she watched him. This morning he was dressed, thank heavens. He was wearing faded jeans and an ancient smoky blue T-shirt, but his simple clothes only served to enhance his rather magnificent broad shoulders, his narrow hips and his long legs.

He was something of a puzzle.

His hut was poor, but he didn't exactly look like a wild man. His clothes were shabby, but his hair seemed to be expertly barbered. It was nice hair, mid-brown in colour, short and thick with a tendency to curl. She suspected that in sunlight the tips would be light, almost blond.

And somehow, despite the very domesticated task of cooking, he managed to look incredibly rugged and masculine.

He turned and saw she was awake. Against the gloomy interior of the hut his eyes were an amazing blue, the colour of an Alpine lake in high summer.

'Good afternoon,' he said.

'Afternoon? What time is it?'

He smiled. 'Only teasing. It's a bit after eight. So you slept OK?'

'Very well, thank you. Your bed is surprisingly comfortable.'

She swung her legs over the edge of the bed and stood carefully. Her head hurt only slightly, and her back was a little stiff, but otherwise she didn't feel too bad.

She sent a swift, anxious glance around the hut. 'May I use your bathroom?'

His eyebrows lifted. 'Sure.'

'Where is it?'

'Outside.' He cocked his head towards the rain-splashed window.

'Out in the rain?'

''Fraid so. This isn't exactly the Ritz, you know.'

She wanted to groan in protest, but just in time she remembered her manners and, clutching his huge shirt around her bare legs, took a tentative step towards the door.

'It's primitive,' he warned, 'like everything out here.'

'*How* primitive is it?'

'It's not too bad. Just like this hut, but much smaller. No flushing system, of course.' He unhooked an oilskin coat from a nail on the wall and held it out to her. 'Here, put this on or you'll get my only spare shirt soaked.'

As she took the coat she had to ask, 'Will—will there be spiders out there?'

One corner of his mouth lifted. 'Sure. You should always check under the seat for redbacks.'

'Red—redbacks?'

'Little black beggars with a red stripe on their rump. They're deadly.'

Deadly! She couldn't bear this. 'What—what do I do if I see one?'

'Kill it. Take a shoe with you and hit it hard.'

He must have seen the sheer dread in her face, because he added, 'But you can yell for help if you really have to.'

'Th-thanks.'

'Keep an eye out for centipedes, too. This wet weather will bring all sorts of creepy-crawlies looking for shelter.'

'Oh, mercy.' Isabella shrank away from him. Could she do this? Could she really go out there? Her knees were shaking so badly she could hardly walk.

Jack stared at her and his eyes narrowed. 'Are you frightened of spiders?'

'I—I'm not used to them.'

'Where do you come from?'

'Amoria. Have you heard of it?'

'Yes,' he said. 'It's that pint-sized country tucked away in the mountains somewhere between France and Spain, isn't it?'

She nodded.

'Surely you have spiders?'

'Our creepy-crawlies are very well behaved. They stay in the forests.' *Or the servants deal with them.*

At the thought of servants, Isabella squared her shoulders. She'd spent a lifetime protected by maids and footmen, but if the recent turmoil in her life had taught her anything, she'd learned that it was time to grow up. To take care of herself.

'If I can get myself out of a flooded car in a creek, I imagine I can look a redback spider in the eye.'

'That's the spirit, Carmen.' Jack continued to stare at her and she couldn't be sure if his eyes were laughing at her. 'You'll be fine,' he said, more gently.

'Yes, I will. I'll be perfectly fine.' Grabbing the coat, she hauled it on and dashed out into the rain before she lost her nerve.

CHAPTER THREE

ISABELLA was hungry.

Jack noted with surprise that she wolfed down three sausages, two eggs, plus toast. At this rate he'd be out of food in no time.

'That was wonderful,' she enthused as she took her plate to the sink, and then she turned and beamed at him as if she'd been struck by a brilliant idea. 'Can I do the washing up for you?'

'Sure,' he said. 'I've heated some water and the detergent's in that squeeze bottle.' He glanced towards the tangle of sheets where she'd slept. 'Were you thinking of making your bed?'

'Oh.' She looked shame-faced. 'Yes, of course. I forgot.'

'And I guess you forgot about all your wet clothes, too.' He let his eyes drift to the sodden heap that she'd left lying on the floor at the foot of her bed. 'I know this hut's not the Taj Mahal, but there's no need to turn it into a pigsty.'

'I'm sorry,' she said, looking stricken. 'What should I do with the clothes?'

He blinked. 'What do you normally do with wet clothes?'

She blushed. 'I—' With a shrug, she said, 'I wash them, of course. But you don't have a washing machine, do you? Or a dryer?'

Jack snorted. Trust him to be saddled with an airhead. 'I've got a bucket, water and soap,' he told her. 'And I can string a fishing line in the corner of the hut for a clothes line.'

Half an hour later he stood at the window, staring grimly out at the grey wall of driving water. 'This rain looks really set in, like proper wet season rain. It could go on for days.'

Behind him, Isabella finished hanging her washed clothes over the fishing line and came to stand beside him. Her hands, damp and pink from washing, rested on her hips. He had to admit that once she turned her mind to domestic tasks she did a pretty good job.

She was still wearing his shirt, and her uncombed hair lay about her shoulders in a black, glossy, just-got-out-of-bed tumble. It should have looked messy, not sexy, but to his dismay looking at Isabella was fast becoming a guilty pleasure, almost an addiction.

'Surely the rain will have to stop soon?' she asked, and scowled at the sheets of water. 'Isn't the Australian Outback supposed to be hot, dry and dusty?'

'Not in the middle of the monsoon season. You didn't do much research before you set off on your travels, did you?'

Her jaw jutted stubbornly. 'If it rained like this in Amoria the entire country would wash down the mountains into Spain.'

'Yeah? Well, sometimes it only takes one night of heavy rain to cause flooding in these parts. If the catchment areas have had a lot of rain, the creeks around here fill up quickly and then no vehicles can get through.' An inexplicable tightness dammed his throat as he added, 'We could be cut off for some time.'

'But I can't stay here.' Her cheeks flushed faintly. 'I can't impose on you. Isn't there some way I can get out?'

'If the weather gets too bad the police will send out a helicopter to check if anyone's in trouble.' He shrugged, making the movement carefully casual. 'Don't worry, as soon as there's a break in the rain I can mark out rocks on the ground to catch their attention and let them know you need airlifting out.'

'By the police?'

An unmistakable flash of fear flickered in her big dark eyes. Jack frowned. Why should the mention of police make her look suddenly scared? 'Don't tell me you're on the run from the law?'

She didn't answer, but stood looking down at her hands while she massaged the cuticles of her left hand with her right thumb.

'For Pete's sake, I'm not harbouring a criminal, am I?'

'Of course not,' she cried, slapping her hands to her sides and looking him straight in the eye. 'No, Jack. I promise you. I swear I'm not a criminal.'

'Well, come on,' he said, his impatience rising. 'You can't leave it at that. If you're not on the run, why are you so uptight at the thought of the police finding you?'

She drew in a sharp breath. 'If you don't mind too much, I'd rather not say.'

'If I don't mind?' he repeated, his voice scathing. 'Cut the hoity-toity politeness, thank you. Of course I mind. I mind very much. If I'm stuck with you here, I'd like to know who you are.'

But it was clear her mind was working on a different wavelength. 'While I'm here, no one will be able to find me, will they?'

'No,' he agreed, frowning at her. *She really was hiding from someone. Hell!* 'That's beside the point,' he growled. '*I* know you're here. You're sleeping in my bed, eating my food. I have a right to know who you are.'

She sighed heavily. 'I admit that you do
have a right to know about me,' she said. 'But
I'm sorry, I have to protect my rights, too. I
have to think about my safety.'

His arms flung wide to proclaim his inno-
cence. 'Isn't it perfectly obvious you're safe
with me?'

'It's not especially obvious. I don't know
anything about you,' she said, just as sharply.

He made a startled grunt of protest, but she
ignored him and continued.

'You've been very good to me, and I'm extremely grateful, Jack, but I don't know how
far I can trust you. I don't even know your full
name.'

What a cheek! Why should he tell a woman
on the run from the law who he was? Heaven
knew what stunt a beautiful felon might pull
if she discovered his identity.

'You're right,' he growled, annoyed to find
himself trapped by her logic. 'I'm no more prepared to trust you than you are to trust me.'
He sighed impatiently. 'I guess that means we
have a stalemate.'

She nodded, but she looked as unhappy as he felt, and she went back to the bench and began to tidy the cooking utensils with nervous, quick movements. Jack stared out into the rain, seething.

First and foremost he was angry with this stranger's secrecy. It was bad enough having her here—but if she was in trouble he deserved to know. He watched the raindrops hitting the muddy ground outside with sharp, bouncy splashes like hundreds, thousands—billions of tiny water bombs. He wondered how high the creek was now. How long would they be stuck here?

Perhaps it was better not to know who this woman was. That way he wouldn't have to deal with the consequences.

Problem was, it wasn't only her secrecy that bothered him. He was angered by her air of vulnerability. And her haunting European beauty. He didn't want her around. She stirred his blood and he didn't want to be stirred. He didn't want to be locked away in a hut in the rain with a beautiful woman.

Not now. Not *this* of all weeks.

This week was for Geri.

He spun on his heel, strode over to his pack and pulled out two thick paperback novels. 'We should make the most of the bad weather. Our conversation doesn't seem to be going anywhere.'

She murmured thanks as she picked up the book he tossed onto the bed, then turned it over and studied the plot summary on the back cover.

'It might not be to your taste,' he admitted. 'It's very much a bloke's book, but that's all I've got.'

'No, it's fine,' she said. 'I like reading all kinds of books.'

To his surprise, she glanced away quickly and gave an abrupt little laugh, as if she'd suddenly thought of something that tickled her funny bone.

'What's the joke?'

'Oh, n-nothing,' she said, growing pink.

His simmering temper peaked. Did this girl have to keep everything a secret? 'Come on,' he urged. 'I've put a roof over your head. You can at least share one joke with me.'

'You won't think this one is funny.'

'Try me. I have an excellent sense of humour.'

Her expressive eyes signalled her big doubts about that possibility, then she blushed again. 'It's just that this whole situation feels so corny.'

'Corny?'

'Like a Hollywood movie—except that if it was a movie...'

Jack waited.

'This is embarrassingly silly, but it—it occurred to me that if this was a Hollywood movie the stranded couple wouldn't be reading books, they'd be too busy falling in love.' Then her face glowed brighter than a red sunset. 'I can't believe I actually said that.'

'I can't believe I forced you to,' Jack muttered. A wave of unexpected heat arced between them and he drew in a sharp, angry breath.

'I'm so sorry. It's just that—'

'It's just that this isn't Hollywood,' he finished through gritted teeth. 'We're in *my* hut and *I* get to write our script.' His voice was as heavy and black as his anger. 'Happy reading.'

Then he veered quickly away to the far side of the room, slumped down onto the fold-out stretcher and prayed that his book would be good enough to help him forget about her for an hour or two.

Isabella read as if her life depended on it. She lay stiffly on the bed and stared grimly at the pages, turning them at regular intervals. She was quite used to reading in English, but for ages nothing on the page made sense. All she could think about was her stupid gaffe.

How on earth had she said something like that to Jack? She'd been trained to speak carefully and behave appropriately in all kinds of social situations, to be discreet and tactful, diplomatic, caring, polite...*modest*.

She turned another page, dimly aware that the story was some kind of action adventure with lots of male characters. Jack was right about it being a bloke's book. She preferred stories with at least one or two females to provide a woman's perspective and perhaps a love interest. Oh, no...there she went again. Her mind had become a one-way track.

With a deep sigh, she put the book down.

The really silly thing was that she actually cared what Jack thought of her. Why? They were mere strangers whose lives were touching briefly. As soon as she could she would leave him in peace.

She shivered and felt a stirring of panic as she turned her thoughts away from Jack to what might be happening back at home. How much time did she have? How long would it be before her fiancé found her?

She could imagine the widespread panic when they discovered she had vanished. Her father would be worried, but Radik would be beyond furious. He would have summoned the Director of Amoria's Bureau of Investigations. Interpol would be involved.

But how long would it take for them to track her down? She let her gaze wander over her surroundings. Would it occur to Amorians that their princess might escape from marriage to the Count of Montez by fleeing to a shabby hut cut off by floods in the Australian Outback?

It was unlikely.

She should be safe here. Yesterday she'd driven deeper and deeper into the Outback, and the sense of physical isolation had been overwhelming. But as the plains had stretched behind her, and the distant mountains and scrub had closed in, she'd felt a sense of sanctuary too—the same sense of safety she'd felt as a child when she crawled beneath her blankets to hide from bedroom monsters.

In reality, the hut's isolation was a blessing. This location was in one of the most sparsely populated places in the world. It was about as safe as she could possibly be.

If she didn't dwell on thoughts of snakes and spiders, scorpions and leeches…and if she stopped saying stupid things to Jack…she could be very safe, even happy here. For a day or so…

*   *   *

Jack stared at his book without seeing a word. He was thinking about Geri. This week marked the third anniversary of her death. That was why he'd come here to Pelican's End—not to dwell on the fact that she'd died, but to remember her life, her passion, her intelligence and her intensity for living.

For the past three years he'd worked hard, harder than was sensible, trying to keep his grief at bay. Finally, when he'd been on the brink, his doctor had insisted that he take a break. Time out.

Time to remember.

So he'd come here, to the place they'd both loved so much. And now this stranger had intruded on his peace, which meant that memories of his wife were more important than ever.

He'd met Geri at university. She'd been writing her honours thesis in Zoology and he'd been completing a Masters in Agricultural Science. Her flaming red hair had caught his attention first, and then he'd discovered that she had a passionate, fiery spirit to match and they'd become lovers almost immediately.

Once they'd completed their university studies their independent career ambitions had caused friction. Geri had been a fighter. Oh, yeah. But eventually they'd reached a compromise, adapting their need to be together to the demands of their jobs.

They'd married and set up a home base in Perth, and had returned there as often as their work allowed. But although Geri had been away for long stretches of time, pursuing her passion for her research and her growing interest in wildlife photography, she'd changed once she fell pregnant.

She'd planned to be an at-home mother when their baby arrived.

Thinking about that was the worst. His throat grew raw and knotted as he remembered how thrilled Geri had been when her petite figure had become increasingly distended with advanced pregnancy. And she'd been ecstatic when she'd developed nesting instincts.

'I'm just like a mother bird,' she'd chirped as they'd painted and decorated the nursery together.

Damn. Tears threatened. He mustn't break down. Not with this other woman lying a few metres away. Double-damn. Even way out here at Pelican's End he couldn't find the space he needed to remember and to think.

Wiping his sleeve over his face, he forced his attention back to the words on the page in front of him, but he was distracted again as Isabella jumped from the bed and ran to the window.

'It's stopped raining!' she cried.

He lowered his book, boosted off his bed and came to join her. 'About time.'

'There's even a little break in the clouds.' She turned to him, her face bright with excitement. 'Can we go outside?'

He nodded. 'Sure. Let's get out before cabin fever sets in.'

The ground outside was squelchy beneath their feet, and water continued to drip and plop from the hut's roof and from nearby trees. The humid air pressed close, smelling of dank earth and vegetation.

'This is lovely,' said Isabella.

She'd had no idea what to expect, and was surprised to discover that Jack's hut was built on top of a high, gently sloping bank overlooking a little lake. The lake's grey surface reflected the sullen rain clouds that still blanketed the sky, but its moody, smoky waters seemed to be home to hundreds of waterbirds—herons, pelicans, wild ducks and geese. On the far side, pale cliffs rose majestically from a base of soft, hazy blue-green bush.

Yesterday, when she'd driven down the highway from Darwin, she hadn't been very enchanted by the harsh, almost frightening Australian landscape. But the bush that circled this little lake was different—nothing like the pine-clad mountains surrounding the lakes at home, of course, but it was clean and fresh from the rain, with its own brand of unique, if untidy beauty.

'I thought the Outback was all barren and harsh, but this is truly beautiful.'

'We call it Pelican's End.'

'I can see why. There are so many birds. It's amazing.'

He nodded. 'I came here for the birdlife. I wanted to photograph them.' He squinted at the sky. 'But we should make the most of this break in the weather to check out the creek first. We can see how your car has fared. I might be able to tow it out with my ute.'

'Ute? What's that?'

'A utility truck. It's parked round the back, behind the hut.'

Without waiting to see her reaction he set off through the rain-sodden scrub. 'Be careful,' he called over his shoulder. 'The track's very slippery.'

The narrow, winding track was indeed slippery, and there were several times when Isabella had to grab at the branches of saplings to retain her balance. She was surprised to discover how far she'd come on her own through the bush last night. It was a miracle she hadn't lost her way. From ahead of them came the roar of rushing water.

Jack came to an abrupt halt and turned back to her, his eyes wide with shock. She hurried to join him and her jaw dropped when she saw the track disappearing into a wide, swirling brown mass of water. There was no sign of her car.

He released a low whistle. 'That's a creek with attitude. How the hell did you escape? I've never seen it this high.'

'It wasn't this high last night,' she murmured. There was no way she could have fought her way out of that maelstrom. 'I must have a guardian angel.'

'And a good deal of courage,' he added.

'I don't think I was very brave. I was panicking and screaming for help.' Isabella shivered as she watched the brown tide hurtle past, and felt ill at the thought that her body could be lying trapped beneath all that ghastly whirling water.

'We won't be able to salvage any of your things.'

'No.'

'And even if there's no more rain it'll be several days before any kind of vehicle will be able to cross here.'

'So I'm stuck here?'

He didn't reply, but his jaw squared with displeasure.

'I really am sorry to be imposing on you like this, Jack. If I had a choice—'

'You'll be able to get out when the police chopper turns up.'

'Well, yes...' she said softly.

There was a lengthy silence while they both stood there, caught up in their thoughts as they stared at the floodwaters. Isabella's thoughts were mostly concentrated on praying that the helicopter stayed away. Police would feel compelled to report her whereabouts to Amorian authorities.

Jack released a long, deep sigh. 'Let's go back and have some lunch. There's no point in hanging around looking at this depressing sight.'

They ate bread and cheese, sitting on a towel spread on a log outside the hut and watching the birdlife on the water. At first Isabella tried to insist that she wasn't hungry. This morning she'd realised that the hut wasn't Jack's permanent home, and that he'd only brought enough food for himself for a short stay, but when she tried to refuse lunch he was adamant that he wouldn't allow her to go hungry.

'I can always catch fish if we run out of food,' he said, and he sounded so certain she believed him.

The rain held off, although the sky remained leaden and heavy with grey clouds.

'This is such a pretty lake,' she said again.

Jack squinted at the clouds. 'Actually, this soft light is rather interesting. I might grab my camera and try for a few shots now, before it decides to rain again.'

He disappeared back into the hut and emerged quite soon with a small backpack and a camera.

'You have a Hasselblad?'

'Yeah.' He slipped its strap around his neck. 'You know about cameras, then?'

'A little. Are you a professional photographer?'

'No way. Photography's just a hobby. This used to belong to—to—' Pain passed over his face like a shadow. 'Someone left it to me.'

Good manners prevented her from prying. She sensed a barrier around Jack, a silent wall of private sadness, and she could tell he wanted it that way.

'You go and take your photos,' she said, not wanting to encroach on his life more than necessary. 'I'll be happy pottering around the lake, and I can always read some more of my book.'

He stared out across the stretch of grey water. 'I'd like to take the canoe. It's better to photograph waterbirds from a boat, because I can keep a lower profile and I'm less likely to scare them away.' He shot a sharp glance her way. 'You'll be OK here, won't you?'

'Yes—sure.' She tried to sound nonchalant. She told herself that Jack wouldn't be gone for long and she was perfectly safe, but unexpectedly she felt a stab of panic at the thought of being left alone in this strange wild place. With a shock she realised that her sense of security in the Outback was disturbingly fragile. It depended on how close she was to this man.

Her attempt to hide her concern must have failed, because his eyes narrowed and he frowned at her. 'You can come with me if you want to,' he said.

It wasn't so much an offer as a statement of fact, but she didn't need a second invitation. 'I'd really like that.'

Relief and excitement skittered through her as she helped him to haul a waterlogged tarpaulin off the canoe and to slide it down the bank to the water's edge. Jack held it steady while Isabella stepped in and took the seat in the bow, then he handed her a paddle before he took the rear seat and pushed off from the bank.

'Do you know what to do?' he called.

She'd actually done quite a bit of canoeing on the lakes at home. 'Like this?' she asked, sweeping her blade smoothly through the water.

'That's it. Terrific!'

She felt a little spurt of pride as they glided out across the silky surface of the lake, and that feeling was quickly followed by a surge of elation, a wonderful sense of freedom.

Her recent ordeals, the escape from Amoria, the long plane flight and the equally long drive from Darwin had been bad enough, but after last night's accident and the cramped conditions in the hut, to be surrounded by fresh air and space and to be out on the water felt as if she'd been given a reprieve from a harsh jail sentence.

No doubt she was very foolish to feel so happy. But the thought of her pursuers hot on her trail couldn't suppress her sense of enjoyment. All her life she'd been crowded—by her family, servants, bodyguards, the public. Now, to be completely alone in an isolated world with just one other human being was like a gift from a good fairy.

She would worry about Amoria when the creek went down. Or when the police helicopter came…

'Stop paddling,' Jack called softly, and she quickly pulled her oar out of the water and rested it on the canoe's rim.

A patch of sunlight had broken through the storm clouds and lit a path across the water,

picking out the snowy white back of a tall wa-
terbird in the shallows. It was standing very
still, its elongated neck poised as it stared
down into the water with its head angled to
one side.

She held her breath, aware of Jack behind
her hurriedly getting his camera ready. As they
watched the great white bird speared its head
beneath the surface in a lightning stroke that
didn't make so much as a ripple. She heard a
soft cry of delight from Jack and the click of
his camera.

When it raised its head once more there was
complete silence, except for the distant quack-
ing of ducks in the reeds near the shore. Then,
at the very instant she heard another quiet click
of the camera shutter, the bird flapped its great
wings and took off.

'Did you catch him?' she asked, turning
back.

'I'm not sure,' he said, and he grinned ruefully. 'It doesn't matter. Photographing birds
is mostly a matter of near-misses. You end up

with the subject too small, or too dark, or out of focus, or with bits of foliage in the way.'

'But every so often you get a perfect shot?'

'Yeah.'

Isabella smiled and Jack smiled back. Their gazes held and she was helplessly trapped by the magnetic blue of his eyes. Against the backdrop of colourless water and subdued bush he looked heart-stoppingly alive. Brutally handsome. Suntanned, rugged, and beautiful in an essentially masculine way.

She felt her heart lift and thud. A pulse in her neck began to beat fast, and then faster still, mimicking the swift beat of the bird's wings when it had lifted away from the water.

Heavenly stars, she was so overcome she couldn't breathe. She'd never felt this way before, not even when Radik had been at his most debonair and charming. It was silly. Jack had made it clear that he tolerated her presence with great reluctance, and yet she wanted him to like her. Very much.

He was the first to break the gaze that bound them. He dropped his chin and his mouth turned grim as he picked up his paddle and gave a curt nod to their right. 'Let's go over closer to the cliffs.'

'Sure.' Isabella kept her eyes firmly in front as she dipped her paddle once more. And as they continued around the lake she made sure she didn't look at Jack again. Heaven knew, there was absolutely no point in getting caught up in girlish romantic fantasies about an anti-social loner who would no doubt be horrified if he knew her real identity.

She focused her attention on the scenery and her paddling. And her problems. She had to work out how she could continue on to her destination without transport or money.

CHAPTER FOUR

THAT evening the ground and kindling were still too wet for a fire, so Jack carried the gas ring outside and they toasted their bread on the end of long forks he'd fashioned from pieces of wire.

'This is so much fun,' Isabella said as she held her toast to the flame.

Her eyes glowed with transparent delight and she looked as excited as she had when they were out on the water. Jack snatched his gaze away. She looked as happy as a child at a fairground. Since when had making *toast* become one of life's big thrills?

He stared out to the sky above the lagoon, where the evening star was making a brave effort to shine through the lingering layers of cloud, and he tried to remember if Geri had been as excited about the meals they'd shared when he'd brought her out here. But her focus

69

had always been on the birds and capturing the perfect photograph.

If Geri had been here now she would have abandoned the toasting fork for her camera. She'd be stalking the ducks and geese that were darting back and forth across the water in frantic search of last-minute snacks before retiring to their roosts.

'Hey, Jack, eat up. This tastes so-o-o good.'

Isabella had piled heated-up tinned curry onto their toast. As he turned to her she tipped her head back to wipe spilled food from her chin, and the movement made her dark hair fall silkily down her back, exposing the pale curve of her throat. He picked up his plate and began to eat quickly.

'I've always wondered what it would be like to live on simple food,' she said between mouthfuls.

He frowned at her strange comment. 'I take it you only get to eat fancy stuff?'

Colour flashed along her cheekbones and she dropped her gaze. 'I—I guess I dine out a lot.'

'Well, if you're looking for a change you're in luck. You'll only get simple fare here.' He finished his curry and toast and picked up a tin of pears. 'These do for dessert?'

'Absolutely.'

He attacked them with a can opener. 'I think I was right when I christened you Carmen.'

She looked up again, her expression puzzled. 'I don't understand that. Why *do* you call me Carmen?'

'Well…you turned up here, coming in from the storm, with long dark hair and big dark eyes, fainting at my feet and mumbling gibberish, and you made me think of a gypsy. Carmen was the first name that popped into my head. And here you are now, enjoying the outdoors and a makeshift campfire. Are you sure you're not some kind of gypsy?'

She flushed quickly and flicked her gaze abruptly away from him to stare up at the starry sky.

'Have I said something wrong?'

'No,' she said, turning his way once more. 'You just made me remember something I'd almost forgotten.' She sighed deeply. 'I'm not a gypsy, but I rather fancy the idea of being a girl called Carmen. Actually, I love it.'

As if to prove the point, she speared her fork into the can of pears Jack offered her, tossed her hair again and tipped her head back as she lowered the juicy fruit into her open mouth. A trickle of pear juice ran down her chin and she laughed as she used a finger to catch it.

Jack watched the performance, and he also watched the movements of her creamy throat as she swallowed and felt the unwelcome throb of desire.

She speared another piece of pear, but before she ate it she said, 'I'm sure Carmens have more fun.'

'I thought it was blondes who were supposed to have more fun.'

'Well, yes, I've heard that too.' She gave him the full benefit of her warmest smile. 'Perhaps it's blondes *and* Carmens. Between them they grab all the fun.'

'And what happens to Isabellas?'

'Isabellas…' Her smile faded and she turned away from him and stared out into the gathering darkness. 'Isabellas have to be careful. Too careful for fun.'

'You reckon?' Jack couldn't resist teasing her. 'So there's no fun for a girl who wears Yves Saint Laurent lingerie?'

The startled and prudish look on her face surprised him.

'You left your underwear hanging all over the place,' he hastened to explain. 'Wasn't hard to miss.'

Neither of them mentioned the fact that he'd removed some of that underwear last night, but the knowledge hovered between them.

Annoyed with himself for broaching such a volatile subject, Jack quickly grabbed another topic. 'So, tell me why being an Isabella isn't much fun.'

She shrugged.

'What kind of work do you do?'

'I—I work in hospitals.'

'As a nurse?'

'No, I'm not a nurse, exactly. My work is mostly to do with charity.'

'Fundraising? Sponsorship?'

'Yes—among other things. What about you, Jack?' she asked, quickly deflecting his curiosity. 'What do you do?'

He almost fabricated an answer—*any* answer—but he was getting a little annoyed by the way they both kept tiptoeing around the truth. 'I'm head of a cattle company.'

'Head? Goodness, that sounds important.'

He nodded.

'Whereabouts?'

'All over. My company has holdings spread across the country, but I have an office and a house in Perth, in Western Australia. I get back there fairly often.'

'So are you with one of those huge companies that produce millions of cattle?'

'Not millions,' he replied guardedly. 'Although we're building all the time.'

'I don't understand why your holdings are spread out? Wouldn't it be better to consolidate in one place?'

'Not really—not if you want to diversify and stay competitive.'

'So you have more than one breed of cattle?'

'Yes—and one part of the country is more suitable for breeding Brahmans, for example, and another area suits Santa Gertrudis. Then once the calves are weaned we send them on to fattening properties in other areas. And if the seasons are bad in one part of the country we can shift the cattle around.'

'It sounds like big business.'

'It is.'

'So is your pastoral company like the Kingsley-Lairds'?'

He felt a slam of shock and frowned. 'You know them?'

'Yes.'

'Honestly?'

'I first met John and Elizabeth Kingsley-Laird in England, and then they visited Amoria last year,' she said, but she looked suddenly worried, as if she was anxious to drop this subject. That suited Jack. Their conversation was getting a little too close to the bone. Any way he looked at it, talking to Isabella was damned difficult. It was like trying to dodge landmines.

She slapped at a mosquito on her arm and he jumped to his feet. 'We'd better go back inside for coffee. Once night starts to fall the insects bombard anyone outside.'

Together they gathered up their things. 'The lantern should be good enough to read by,' he said. 'How's your book going?'

'It's excellent,' she answered hastily, but he suspected she was lying.

'I'm just getting to the big climax in mine.' He was definitely lying, but he was pretty damn sure that reading until he fell asleep was the safest thing he could do tonight.

Before breakfast next morning, Isabella felt brave enough to set off around the lake to find a secluded cove where she could bathe. The day was already warm, but the water was cool and surprisingly clear, and she let herself float, staring up at the sky.

A flight of herons winged overhead, their long necks stretching forward like miniature jets, and a mere handful of fluffy flat-bottomed clouds sat low on the horizon like floating islands. The rest of the pale blue heavens were as clear and clean as a freshly laundered tablecloth.

She laughed aloud. What would Toinette, her maid, think if she could see her princess bathing in the outdoors, protected by nothing but a fringe of reeds and a stern-eyed pelican?

She would probably be even more shocked if she could see her living alone with a man. A tall, lean, gorgeous man. Not a hermit, but a successful king of the Outback.

She hadn't been too surprised to learn that Jack was the CEO of a huge cattle company. He was the kind of man people noticed and obeyed. But she wished she'd asked him what he was doing here at Pelican's End. Was he hiding too? It was strange that, despite the mystery that surrounded him, she felt she could trust him. She was safe with him.

After she was dry, and had changed back into her own clothes, she felt deliciously clean and invigorated and ready to face the day ahead. There were all sorts of things she should be worrying about, but it was hard to focus on anything beyond the beauty of the morning and the simple pleasure of drying her hair in the sun.

The world was so quiet and peaceful here. Her fears about the past and the future faded as she drank in the innocent beauty of now. Here, by the lake, it was easy to imagine that her problems could be put on hold indefinitely.

They breakfasted on fried tomatoes and the last of Jack's sausages, followed by tea, toast and ginger marmalade. While they ate they watched squadron after squadron of black shags fly in over the lake, skimming so close to the water their wings almost touched its surface.

Isabella was so absorbed in watching the birds that at first she took no notice of the pulsing throb-throb-throbbing sound in the distance.

But Jack looked towards the horizon and frowned. 'Sounds like the police chopper's on its way,' he said.

Her toast fell to the dirt.

So soon?

Her heart began a fearful knocking and her stomach clenched as she scanned the sky. A tiny speck hovered in the distance. 'Are you sure it's the police?'

'There's a very good chance.' Without another word Jack set down his mug and jumped to his feet.

The black dot moved relentlessly towards them, and Isabella felt so panicky she wanted to dash inside the hut and hide. But it was more important to stop Jack from attracting the police.

'I'm going to signal them down,' he shouted, and rushed towards the lake. 'Quick—come and give me a hand.'

'No,' she cried, hurrying after him. 'Jack, please don't wave at them.'

'Don't be ridiculous,' he yelled over his shoulder. 'You can't hide here for ever.'

'You don't understand.'

'You're dead right,' he yelled. He swung back and glared at her. 'I've Buckley's chance of understanding you because you won't tell me a damned thing.'

She tried to grab his elbow, but he yanked it free. 'You can't turn me over to the police.'

His blue eyes burned. 'Why the hell not?'

'It's dangerous for me.' She heard the panic in her voice and knew that he must have noticed it too. 'Please believe me.'

For a moment he hesitated, and in the sudden stillness the sound of the approaching aircraft loomed. His gaze flickered to the sky, then back to her. 'Sorry, sweetheart. You've had plenty of time to explain your problem, but now you've lost your chance.'

He raised his hands above his head.

Isabella screamed, 'If you send me back to Amoria I'll die!'

'For God's sake!' Jack leapt at her and grabbed her shoulders so hard his fingers dug into her flesh. He glared at her as if he wanted to shake her. 'You've got one last chance,

Carmen. Tell me exactly who you are, and why you're here, or I stand here waving and jumping up and down till they see us.'

She threw a frantic glance to the sky. The helicopter was a big black blot against the sun, growing bigger every moment. 'Come inside the hut quickly and I'll tell you.'

'No! Tell me here. Now. Hurry.'

'They'll see us! Please, come!'

'Tell me, Isabella!'

Panic flared. Already there wasn't time to reach the hut.

'Do you promise to believe me?'

'Yes. Of course. Stop wasting time.'

'I'm a princess.'

Jack's head jerked forward as he gaped at her. 'You're a *what*?'

'Princess Isabella of Amoria.'

'Like hell you are.'

But Isabella wasn't waiting another second. 'Let's go,' she shouted, and she turned and dashed into the nearby trees, her heart thumping so hard it seemed to hit her throat.

Once she reached cover she turned to see Jack standing, staring after her, still frozen with shock. 'Jack!' she screamed. 'Come on. Please, hide!'

She hurried deeper into the bush, and at last, behind her, she heard the crashing and thumping that told her that he was following. Ducking low, she crouched beneath a dense shrub with silvery leaves.

Above them the loud clatter of the helicopter thundered.

'Down here,' she called to Jack, and the next minute he was beside her.

In the crowded space beneath the leaves Jack's hard, muscular arm and thigh crammed against hers. Their hiding place smelled of damp earth and crushed eucalypt leaves. And Jack. He shouldn't have smelled good. She shouldn't have been noticing how Jack smelled.

Sharp branches were poking into her hair and back, and her heart was pounding so fiercely it might well have been competing with the overhead throb of the helicopter. And yet she was noticing that Jack smelled of shaving soap and manly perspiration.

'Did I hear you right?' he shouted close to her ear. 'Did you say you were a princess?'

'Yes.'

'A proper blue-blood member of a royal family?'

'Yes,' she repeated, and was surprised to hear the note of apology in her voice. 'My father is King Albert of Amoria.'

Above them the helicopter's roar lessened as it arced away to circle the lake.

'And you're running for your life?'

'I'm afraid so.' She peered through the overhead tangle of leaves and branches, trying to see the chopper, but she could only catch frustrating tiny glimpses of sky. 'Why are they staying here so long?' she asked as the engine's roar continued on the far side of the lake. 'Do you think they saw us?'

'They wouldn't know I'm out here. They're just checking to see if anyone's in trouble.' He frowned at her. 'Could they be looking for you? Do they know you're here?'

'I don't know,' she said. 'I don't think so. I hope not.'

'But you really believe you're in danger?'

'Yes. And if I went to your police there would be pressure for them to hand me back. It's best that no one knows where I am.'

Jack let out his breath with a whoosh. 'I can't believe this. A runaway princess. It's so crazy. It's surreal.'

She craned her neck, trying to see where the helicopter was now. 'What if they saw the canoe?'

'It shouldn't matter if they're just doing their normal check. Unless they're specifically looking for you they probably won't land, because we haven't signalled that we're in trouble.'

She flashed an anxious glance back to him. 'You're sure?'

'That's how it's always worked in the past.'

Up this close, his eyes were such an indelible blue they made her head spin. 'So if the helicopter moves away, can we assume they don't know about me?'

'I'd say it's a safe bet.' He cleared his throat and cast a hasty glance around them. 'I'm sorry about these cramped conditions.'

He was *sorry*? There was no way she could be sorry to be shoulder-to-shoulder with him, to have the solid length of his thigh pressed so closely against hers. She was tingling all over. 'I don't mind,' she said quickly, and then wondered if that had sounded too much as if she was enjoying herself. 'You don't need to apologise. You're not responsible for the undergrowth.'

After that, neither spoke as they crouched together, waiting for the chopper to move away. When at last it did, Jack crawled forward on his hands and knees and then turned and held out his hand to help her.

She was surprised when he helped to brush the leaves and twigs from her hair and clothes, and although it was nice that he cared, she felt a spurt of irritation. First he'd been apologising; now he felt compelled to assist her. Already his behaviour was changing. He was reacting to the news that she was a princess.

All her life her royal title had shaped the way people treated her, and she couldn't help regretting that she'd had such a brief time to enjoy being plain Isabella. It had been fun.

'OK,' Jack said, once he was satisfied that she was comfortable. 'Let's go back to the hut and you can explain exactly what you're doing here.'

A princess! Jack grappled to wrap his head around the notion. As they walked his gaze kept sliding sideways, as if he needed to check that Isabella still looked the same. It was so hard to believe that this slip of a girl, in wrinkled, unironed clothes, with her untidy hair tied back loosely by a piece of string, was a true-blue Amorian princess.

Who would have thought?

And he'd suggested she might be a gypsy.

Nevertheless, in a roundabout way her claim seemed to make sense. He was surprised by how ready he was to believe her. There was an air of gentility and dignity about her—an otherworldliness—and clues like her luxurious underwear and her fascination with simple food.

Hell…

He felt a flush of heat redden the back of his neck when he thought about the offhand way he'd treated her—chipping her for not making her bed or washing her clothes, sending her off to the outhouse to kill her own spiders, making fun of her underwear…

When they reached the hut he said, 'I need a drink, but all I've got here is tea.'

'Let me make it,' she said quickly.

He fended her off with outstretched palms. 'It's OK. You take a seat.'

Her eyes sent him a dark warning. 'Jack, you don't have to treat me any differently because you know who I am. I don't expect you to start waiting on me.'

He frowned, and turned with a shrug to light the burner. 'I don't mind.'

'I've had a lifetime of being treated like a princess. I've been enjoying the change.'

His eyes made a cursory sweep of the interior of the hut. 'Like the prince and the pauper?'

'I suppose so.' She propped her hip against the bench, crossed her arms over her chest and eyed him levelly. 'Can you promise me one thing?'

'What's that?'

'Whatever you do, don't start calling me Your Highness. I'm still Isabella.'

He laughed. 'No fear on that count. I'm an Australian. We're not big on titles anyway. So, what are your other names? Are you like British royalty—with a string of them?'

Her eyes flashed and her chin lifted to a haughty, very princess-like angle. 'I'm Isabella Mary Damaris Alice Martineau—second in line to the throne of Amoria, behind my brother, the Crown Prince Danior.'

He couldn't help grinning. *She was the genuine article!* 'Isabella-Mary-Something-Alice. All those fancy names and still no Carmen.'

'I don't mind if you want to call me Carmen.'

The vulnerability in her eyes and her timid smile made his chest tighten and his grin fade. Isabella gave a little sigh and moved away.

'Perhaps you'd better tell me your story,' he suggested, and his voice sounded unnecessarily serious. He didn't want her to think he was flirting.

She shook her head. 'You don't want to be burdened with my problems.'

'That's for me to decide. There's no burden in listening.' He set the billy full of water to boil. 'I'm not promising I can help.'

He stood facing her, his hands resting lightly on his hips, his mood intent and expectant, and he could sense the instant that she decided to tell him. One moment she was shaking her head and looking away, her white teeth biting her lower lip, the next her pretty dark eyes had found his and he could see a brief internal struggle and then release.

Almost without emotion, she said, 'My fiancé plans to kill me.'

'Bloody hell.' The exclamation slipped out, but before Jack could apologise Isabella rushed to explain.

'I know it sounds crazy. I had trouble believing it at first.'

'Are you sure he means to harm you?'

'Yes.'

'Why?'

'He views our marriage as a merger. A business venture. All he wants is access to my money and my estates.'

'How did you find this out?'

With quick nervous movements she began to rearrange the tins of food on the bench in front of her. 'A very good friend of mine, Dr Christos Tenni, was at a conference in Geneva and he overheard Radik, the Count of Montez—that's my fiancé—discussing his plans with his lover.'

'The mongrel!'

Isabella swallowed and her hands shook.

Jack stepped towards her, took the tin she was holding and set it aside on the bench, then he captured both her hands in his. He stroked her fingers lightly with his thumb.

For several seconds she looked at her hands in his, and then she glanced up at him from beneath trembling lashes.

'Apparently Radik—that's my fiancé—favours a car crash on a mountain for my demise.'

It seemed so unreal to hear her talking about her own death this way. 'You're not joking, are you?'

'Believe me, I wish I was.'

'I assume this informant, this Dr Tenni, is completely trustworthy?'

Her eyes filled with tears. 'He was my own doctor—but I also worked in his hospital, so I knew him professionally as well. I would never doubt Christos's word. He was a very good friend.'

'You said he *was*—has something happened to him?'

This time the bright tears overflowed and spilled down her cheeks. 'The day after he warned me of my danger—' She pulled a hand from his grasp and pressed it over her mouth as she struggled to hold back sobs. 'Oh, God, Jack.'

His arm slipped around her shoulders, holding her closer. 'What happened?'

Sobbing, she shook her head against him. It took some time and several deep breaths before she could go on. 'It happened the very next day. A hit-and-run accident right in front of the hospital.'

'He was killed?'

'Yes.'

Jack swore under his breath.

'I panicked,' she said in a very small voice. 'My father was away and I lost the nerve to wait. I grabbed my passport and a wig and sunglasses and headed straight for the airport.'

Her words caused an ache in his solar plexus. Damn. Despite his best intentions, he was feeling involved.

As if she'd sensed the sudden tension in him, Isabella pulled out of his arms. 'Look...I'm really sorry to be burdening you with this,' she said.

'What puzzles me is why you wanted to marry this fellow in the first place. You weren't being forced to, were you?'

'In a way I was...'

'I thought arranged marriages were a thing of the past?'

She shrugged. 'At first I thought I really was in love with Radik. He's very handsome and charming.'

'Bully for him.' Jack crossed his arms over his chest. 'But once you found out how utterly lacking in charm he was, couldn't you have called off the wedding?'

'It's hard to explain. You've no idea what happens to a princess as soon as her engagement is announced. I lost all control of my life. A royal wedding is a *huge* deal. In Amoria it felt as if the entire country had an emotional stake in *my* marriage.'

Remembering the ruckus his own wedding had caused, Jack nodded.

Her mouth pulled into a shame-faced grimace. 'I know I'm a coward for running away, but I was so scared. I wasn't sure I could convince my father to call off the wedding. Our relationship is somewhat…strained.' She looked embarrassed. 'I suppose you find that difficult to understand?'

'Not at all.' *I understand more than you could possibly guess.*

She sighed. 'Father and his advisers think the world of my fiancé. And Radik has a smooth tongue. He would have found a way to convince them I'd been misinformed—deluded.'

'And there was no one else you could talk to? No other family or friends?'

Slowly she shook her head. 'Not really. My mother died when I was young. My brother's too absorbed with his studies in England and the stream of hot and cold running blondes flowing to his door. As for my friends—' She shrugged. 'When your father's a king, there's only so much girlfriends can do.'

'So you came down here to escape?'

'Australia is so far away. It seemed the best plan.'

Jack grimaced as he looked around the hut, trying to imagine what it looked like through her eyes. 'You must be finding this accommodation just a little different from home.'

'I'm getting used to it.' She shot a glance towards the cobwebs in the corner. 'Except for the spiders.'

With an uncomfortable throat-clearing growl, he turned to the bench.

'Jack, please understand that just because I've told you all this it doesn't mean I expect you to help me.'

He handed her a chipped enamel mug of tea and she sat on the stool while he used the up-turned petrol drum again. He leaned forward, staring thoughtfully into his mug, and shrugged.

'So when's this wedding supposed to take place?'

'On Saturday.'

'*Saturday?*' He almost dropped his tea. 'Not this Saturday coming?'

'Yes. That's why I freaked. The Amorian papers are full of nothing but the wedding. Half of Europe knows every detail.'

He released a low whistle.

'Trying to stop all that single-handed seemed—'

'Like trying to stop the Olympic Games when the athletes are in the starting blocks?'

'Exactly.'

Jack stared at the floor, with his elbows resting on his knees and his mug of cooling tea cradled in his hands. 'So this Count of Montez will be looking for you, won't he? I imagine he'll be desperate to get you back and get you safely to the altar.'

'I suppose so. I'm trying not to think about that.'

Jack drew in a long, deep breath, then let it out again slowly. 'It's all happening now for you, isn't it?' he said. 'First you get lost. Then you narrowly escape drowning in the flooded creek. You struggle through the bush in the middle of a storm and end up here half dead.' His grin was shaky. 'Isabella, there's more of Carmen in you than you realise.'

She knew this was his way of paying her a compliment, and she felt absurdly pleased.

'But where were you heading when you crashed?' he asked.

'To John and Elizabeth's.'

'The Kingsley-Lairds? You weren't heading for Killymoon, were you?'

Her eyes widened with surprise. 'As a matter of fact, yes, I was. When they left Amoria last year they extended a very kind invitation. And Killymoon is so far away from Amoria, and so isolated, it seemed perfect. Do you know them?' She half expected him to say that he did know the family well.

He didn't meet her gaze, and he seemed to choose his words carefully before he replied. 'There's no doubt the Killymoon homestead would suit your purposes.' He sent another quick, sardonic glance around the hut. 'And it would be a darn sight more comfortable than here.'

She sighed, disappointed by his evasive reply. 'I'd be there now if I hadn't taken that wrong turn in the dark and ended up in the creek.'

'Why didn't you phone the Kingsley-Lairds from Darwin? They would have arranged for a plane to fly you in.'

'Would they?'

'Sure.'

'Do you know them well?'

A shutter seemed to fall over his eyes, shielding his thoughts. 'Well enough.'

'I was so anxious to keep moving and not attract attention that as soon as I got to Darwin I hired a car and hit the highway. I don't know how I'm going to get to Killymoon now.'

'You're already on the property.'

'Really?' She frowned. 'I thought I was still about a hundred kilometres away.'

His mouth tilted in a faint ironic smile. 'You *are* still a hundred kilometres away from the homestead, but Killymoon is a big property. One of the biggest in the world.'

'Good heavens.' She shook her head in amazement. 'It must be bigger than Amoria.'

Jack drained his mug and rose to his feet. Isabella told herself she shouldn't be admiring the way he moved, but although she knew it was totally inappropriate, she found everything about him undeniably impressive. His controlled casualness fascinated her.

'I could take you to Killymoon homestead,' he said, not quite looking at her.

'But how? If the creek is cut we're stuck here, aren't we?'

'We don't have to take the roads. In fact, we're probably better off keeping away from the highway. You never know, your Count might already have people out there, trying to find you.'

'But how else could we get to Killymoon? I don't think I could walk one hundred kilometres in this heat.'

He looked out through the doorway of the hut, and she followed his gaze and saw the canoe pulled up on the lake's shore. 'I wasn't thinking about walking.'

Jumping to her feet, she hurried to stand beside him. 'Are you saying we could take the canoe?'

'That's exactly what I'm thinking. The creek's flowing fast, but not as fast as yesterday, and it's not rising any more. It runs into the Pinnaroo River, which can take us all the way down to Killymoon homestead. With a bit of luck we could be there in two days, three at the outside.'

'But what about your own plans? A trip like that would take up a lot of your time.'

Did she imagine the flickering shadow that seemed to darken his face momentarily?

He shrugged. 'My plans are flexible.'

She might have pursued the question further, but something in his face, his air of calm authority, cautioned her not to push. If Jack didn't want to help her he wouldn't have offered.

He looked at her thoughtfully, as if he were taking her measure. 'Do you think you're up to it?'

'Up to it?'

'How do you feel about canoeing that far?'

'I'd love it,' she said, without hesitating.

'We'd have to camp out overnight. It would mean sleeping in the open.'

She blanched as she tried to squash visions of being eaten by wild animals.

'We'll be OK. I've got mosquito nets,' he said, noting her hesitation.

'I wasn't thinking of mosquitoes. Um—I know you don't have lions and tigers in Australia, but...'

The skin around his eyes creased. 'But?'

'But what about all the snakes and the crocodiles? You have them, don't you?'

'There are freshwater crocodiles around here, but they only eat fish. As for snakes—yeah, we have them, and they'll be hanging around at the moment because of all the rain, but they usually only bother you if you bother them.'

His gaze was unexpectedly gentle, and he touched a finger to her cheek and let it trail down to her chin. 'I wouldn't take you down the river if I thought it was too dangerous. The point of this exercise is to keep you safe.'

Keep you safe.

Those three words, in company with the gentleness of his touch, the kindness in his voice and the steadfast look in his eyes, made her feel so protected she could have cried.

The past few days had been a nightmare, and Jack was fast becoming the hero who'd figured in all her girlhood dreams. Like a storybook knight in shining armour.

'You'll be my hero, Jack,' she said, sending him a smile that was a mixture of coyness and teasing. And she couldn't resist adding, 'Will you be the princess's champion? Can I trust you to take me unharmed through the Valley of the Dragons?'

He looked shocked. 'Don't get carried away. There's nothing romantic about this. I'll take you down the flooded creek to Killymoon, but that doesn't make me Sir Lancelot escorting Guinevere to Camelot.'

Isabella wasn't so sure.

CHAPTER FIVE

THEY ate one last meal on the banks of the lake, looking out over the stretch of water and watching cheeky black shags try to steal fish straight from a pelican's bill. Isabella felt a guilty pang at the thought that she was dragging Jack away from this lovely setting, but if he resented leaving he showed no sign.

They set off straight after lunch, first carrying their gear along the track to the creek and leaving it on the high bank while they went back for the canoe, which also had to be carried.

'Make sure you cover that Alpine complexion of yours with plenty of this,' Jack said, handing her a bottle of sunscreen.

She slathered it on while he stowed everything very carefully in plastic drums in the bottom of the canoe.

'You'd better have this, too,' he said, and he dropped his wide-brimmed akubra hat onto her head.

'But it's yours.'

'My nose isn't as delicate as yours.'

'Well, thanks, but I'm afraid this hat's too big for me.'

To her surprise, he picked up a handful of her dark curls. 'What if we tuck your hair up under it? That should help to keep it on, shouldn't it?'

'Perhaps.'

'Hold still, then.'

It was such a simple thing for Jack to wind her heavy hair into a loose knot and tuck it up inside the hat, yet Isabella hardly knew how to deal with the blaze of warmth that flashed through her. She couldn't remember any time in her life when a man, apart from her hairdresser, had handled her hair in such an intimate way. She was sure her neck must be bright red.

'Shake your head,' Jack instructed, ducking to smile at her beneath the wide brim.

She shook her head carefully, and then a little more vigorously. The hat stayed in place.

'That should do the trick,' he said. 'OK, let's get going.'

Although the creek's current wasn't quite as fierce as it had been, it was still very swift, and Isabella quickly discovered that they had to paddle even faster than the water's flow to maintain control over the canoe.

A rush of adrenalin, more excitement than fear, sent her heart racing, and she had to concentrate on deliberately steadying her breathing and willing her shoulders to relax, so that she could match her strokes to Jack's strong, even paddling rhythm.

Fleeting impressions of the scenery flashed by—thick-trunked trees with peeling white papery bark—thin tapering leaves and branches hanging low over the water like Outback versions of weeping willows. Out of the corner of her eye she caught sight of a red kangaroo, its long tail bouncing behind it as it bobbed through the scrub.

'The current will be slower when we reach the main river,' shouted Jack.

'Don't worry. I'm fine,' she called back over her shoulder. And she meant it. She knew the muscles in her arms and shoulders would be aching by the end of the day, but despite her slender frame she was strong and fit. At home she skied in winter and canoed in summer, and she was savouring every moment now.

But her stomach dropped when they rounded a bend and she saw menacing dark rocks looming out of foaming white water.

'Rapids!' she yelled.

'Pull your paddle in and hang on to your hat,' Jack called back. 'I'll steer us through here.'

For a split second she sensed a prickle of hurt pride. Why couldn't she help? But as the current picked them up and hurled them towards the rocks common sense prevailed. Jack was in the canoe's stern, the best position for driving and steering, and a wrong move from her might capsize them or send them slamming into the basalt. Quickly she pulled her paddle out of the water and held her breath as their light craft catapulted forward.

The angry water tossed them about like a leaf in an autumn wind gust, and she knew that it took all of Jack's stronger muscles and superior skill to keep the canoe clear of the black boulders.

She didn't dare turn back to watch him, but sat very still, holding onto his hat and crouching low so he could see over her. She held her breath as the canoe skipped and skimmed at a reckless pace, dodging danger by mere inches.

And then suddenly they were shooting out into a wider expanse of calmer water.

'This is the junction where the creek joins the Pinnaroo River,' Jack explained. 'How are you holding out?'

She turned back to look over her shoulder and saw the breathtaking blue sparkle of his eyes. He was grinning and she smiled back at him. 'That was very impressive canoeing. I'm having the time of my life, thanks.'

And how true that was. This was like living her personal fantasy—stepping out of the royal spotlight and having her own private adventure. And even though this interlude in the Outback with Jack would only be for a few days, she knew it would leave a lasting legacy. It would be an exciting memory to hold in her heart. At points in the future, when the tedium of life in the public eye got her down, she would be able to remember this.

She had to forget about the threat of Radik and live in *this* moment. Absorb everything.

Now, to the right and left of her stretched a magnificent wide river with tall limestone cliffs on the far side and a huge blue dome of bright sky overhead.

'Now we just keep heading downstream,' Jack said, and his big shoulders rolled smoothly as he lifted his paddle and dug it into the water once more. 'And the further we go down the Pinnaroo, the clearer it will get. All the feeder streams from now on come out of limestone country and are spring fed.'

They settled into an easy paddling pace and the canoe slid happily forward. There was so much to see. Like the lake, the river teemed with birds. Pleased that already she'd learned to identify many of them, she watched with delight as black ducks, pelicans, divers and cormorants swam, dived, frolicked or sat in the sun and spread their wings to dry their feathers.

Each bend in the river brought an exciting new vista.

On the tops of the high banks beautiful gum trees with huge towering white trunks and buttresses of dark brown bark stood sentry. Mobs of silvery-white cattle with big faces, floppy ears and camel-like humps stood in the shade of these trees and seemed to watch the canoe's progress.

The only frustration was that she couldn't see Jack without turning back, so she contented herself with imagining his rippling muscles and the powerful strength in his tanned arms as he paddled. It was fun to pretend they were intrepid explorers, and that the Pinnaroo River was the Amazon or the Nile.

She and Jack were alone in a hot, steamy wilderness.

Tarzan and Jane...

At the next bend the limestone cliffs closed in on both sides, the river narrowed and they shot into a race of fast water that spun them out into a surprisingly clear pool with a sandy bottom and a fringe of shady trees and fan-like palms.

'Are you hot?' Jack called. 'I am. I need a swim.'

She was terribly hot. Beneath the hat, her hair felt damp and itchy, and her shirt stuck to her in wet, sweaty patches. The water looked clean and very cool and inviting. But...

'I don't have a swimming costume.'

She heard Jack's chuckle as he steered for the shore.

Once they were both standing on the bank, he said, 'Pardon me, Princess, but when you're out in the bush you don't stand on ceremony.'

With that he kicked off his shoes, stripped off his shirt, undid his jeans and stepped out of them, letting his discarded clothes fall in a careless tangle on the bank behind him.

Heavenly stars, he was wearing nothing but a brief pair of underpants. But she wasn't so shocked that she didn't appreciate his superbly sculptured, almost naked masculine physique.

Seeing Jack now was a different experience from the night she'd arrived, when she'd caught a terrified glimpse of him in the lamplight. Now, in broad daylight, his big shoulders, smooth brown back, lean hips and long, strong legs sent sexy quivers rippling under her skin.

He shot a winking smile her way. 'Are you going to join me?'

Her hand touched the top button of her blouse. 'I—I don't think so.'

He nodded, as if he understood that there were limits to a European princess's sense of adventure, then strode to the water's edge and dived in—arching, sleek and pure in mid-air, before disappearing head-first beneath the water.

Isabella watched his powerful strokes as he progressed across the pool. Did she dare to follow? The afternoon was so hot, a swim would be perfect. But how could she undress here? Even though Jack had seen her body when he'd removed her wet clothes on that first night, to strip down to her underwear now was a step that seemed too huge to take.

He was already halfway to the far side. Perhaps he was giving her space and relative privacy?

If I'm having an adventure, I should do this. If this were a Hollywood movie...

Why did she keep thinking of Hollywood? Was it because her life was becoming increasingly less real?

She looked out again to where Jack was floating on his back, kicking in a leisurely style and staring up at the sky...not interested in her...not looking her way...

Jack heard the splash and glanced back towards the bank to see rippling circles and then Isabella's dark head emerging above the water.

'Well, I'll be...' he said softly, and he smiled, treading water as he watched her swim towards him with sharp-elbowed, inexpert strokes.

His own breaststrokes were lazy as he swam to meet her halfway. 'What do you think?' he asked when he drew near to her. Her curly hair had been straightened by the weight of the water and fell in dark satiny curtains on either side of her face.

'This pool is beautiful,' she said, laughing. 'I feel so free.' She flicked water into the air and watched the droplets catch the sunlight before falling around her like sparkling diamonds.

'We *are* free here,' he said. 'That's why I love to come out here. We're free as the birds.'

A sudden piping call high above them caught his attention and he looked up to see a pair of grey falcons tumbling and swooping in the air. It was rare to see grey falcons in these parts. They were desert birds. Floating on his back, he squinted to bring them into sharper focus and continued to watch them as they flew to the top a dead gum tree on the far ridge.

'Jack! Help! *Help!*'

Isabella's scream and sudden thrashing sent a bolt of fear ripping through him. In a split second he was at her side. 'What is it? What's the matter?'

She flung her arms around his neck and clung to him, shivering with terror. 'Something touched me,' she cried, and he could feel her heart pounding against his chest. 'Could it be a crocodile?'

'I shouldn't think so.' He couldn't help grinning.

'It's not funny. Oh, God! I have to get out of here.'

She began to pull out of his arms, but as soon as he released her she was seized by panic, thrashed wildly and went under again.

Ducking beneath the water, he caught her around the waist and hauled her high. 'No need to panic,' he told her as she gasped and spluttered. 'I'm here. I've got you. Try to relax and I'll take you to the shore.'

Holding her against his chest, he swam using sidestroke and brought her back to the bank.

'Oh, Jack—oh, dear God,' she sobbed, still clinging to him in the shallows. 'Thank you.'

She huddled there gasping, struggling to steady her breathing. Without speaking Jack held her with her head tucked against his shoulder, and did his best to ignore how perfectly her slim, soft smoothness fitted against him.

After some time she said, 'I'm sorry I panicked, but that was so bad. I hate it when things touch me in the water.'

'Don't apologise,' he said, lifting a strand of wet hair from her cheek. 'I should have warned you. There are all sorts of things in the river—fish, eels, turtles—but nothing really dangerous.'

She lifted her beautiful dark eyes and looked up at him from beneath long lashes glistening with starry water drops.

'It touched my leg,' she said. 'And I've heard so many stories of people being eaten by crocodiles in Australia.'

'The only crocs that eat folk are the salties.'

'Salties?'

'Saltwater crocodiles. Any crocodiles up here would be the freshwater ones.'

'Are you sure?'

'Absolutely. The Pinnaroo Falls are just a few kilometres downstream from Killymoon homestead. No crocs can get past them.' He grinned. 'They can't climb cliffs and they can't swim up waterfalls. Relax. I'm looking after you. I wouldn't be swimming with saltwater crocs.'

He eased his body gently away from hers and hoped she hadn't noticed the embarrassing effect of having her dainty curves so near him. Serve him right for stripping down to next to nothing.

'I've spoiled your swim,' she said.

'Doesn't matter. I've cooled off.' What a joke! He turned away from her, strode towards his jeans and hauled them on over his wet jocks.

Glancing back to Isabella, he saw the way she looked down at herself and her cheeks grew pink, as if she'd just realised how transparent her wet undies were. Turning her back to him, she grabbed up her own clothes.

'I guess we'll dry off quickly once we start paddling again,' she said, looking back at him over her shoulder, while holding her clothes in front of her like a shield.

She'd hooked her long hair over one shoulder, inadvertently exposing her slim, pale back, and Jack found himself noting the perfect line of her backbone, her neat shoulderblades, the delightful roundness of her buttocks.

He turned abruptly and strode away along the riverbank while she dressed. Hell, he needed to think about Geri. He summoned a mental picture of his wife and found himself struggling to remember the exact shape of her back, her shoulderblades, her buttocks.

With a groan he covered his face with his hands and concentrated hard, willing himself to forget this girl and to remember every detail of how his wife had looked, how she'd felt in his arms.

But he couldn't find Geri. Panic threatened, and for frantic seconds he couldn't breathe.

Just when he began to see Geri the image would dissolve. He tried again, and she wouldn't come. A cry of rage erupted from his throat, and he knew if he didn't snap out of it he would give way to tears.

Dragging in a noisy deep breath, he willed himself to get a grip.

When he returned to Isabella she stood stiffly, watching him, her face troubled. 'Jack, I feel so silly now. I hope you don't think I'll need rescuing every time I get a fright on this trip.'

'Of course not,' he said gruffly.

Her cheeks grew pink again. 'I'm sorry I threw myself all over you.'

'Don't give it a second thought. I won't.'

Yeah, right, he thought, making sure his eyes didn't meet hers. With more haste than necessary he moved towards the canoe and pushed it back down the bank to the river.

They kept going until the sun slipped towards the western rim and long shadows stretched across the water.

When at last Isabella stepped onto the shore, at the spot Jack had chosen for their campsite, her arms, shoulders and back were painfully stiff, but as she watched Jack haul the canoe high and dry he showed no signs of discomfort.

She hadn't meant to stare, but she couldn't help herself. There was something about the confident, casual way he did things that kept drawing her attention. While she gathered dry wood for their fire, she kept sneaking peeks at him. He was tying a piece of rope between two trees and stretching a mosquito net across it, and a green lightweight nylon tarpaulin over that.

'It shouldn't rain, but this will keep away stray showers,' he said, squinting quickly up at the cloudless sky. Then he knelt and scraped two body-sized dents in the sandy loam to take their sleeping swags.

She gulped when she saw the two canvas swags, lying so close, side by side. Tonight she would be lying there beside Jack. The thought brought a warm and tightening sensation low inside her.

'Will this be enough timber for our fire?' she asked quickly, needing to switch her attention to safer matters.

Jack shot a quick glance towards the pile of sticks she'd collected and flashed her a sardonic smile. 'That's not a bad start, but we'll need bigger logs to burn down into coals if we want to bake our fish.'

'Right,' she said, using a businesslike voice to cover how silly she felt. No doubt he'd guessed that she'd never collected firewood or baked a fish.

'I'll help you,' he offered.

'It's OK. I can manage,' she snapped crossly, and was instantly sorry for her rudeness. Jack was going out of his way to escort her safely to Killymoon and she had an obligation to be polite in return. 'I'm happy to look for bigger pieces of timber,' she said in a more conciliatory tone. 'You get on with your fishing.'

Once the fire was started, she sat on the sand beside it, with her arms wrapped around her bent knees while she watched Jack bait a hook with an earthworm and throw his line out into the river.

The setting was lovely. The last rays of the dying sun warmed her back and gilded Jack's bronzed, outflung arms, and coated the quiet water with liquid gold. A solitary white heron fished the far bank, moving through the sunlit shallows with slow, focused stealth.

The peaceful scene should have relaxed her and uplifted her spirits. But instead she felt horribly down. Perhaps it was simply her tiredness from the long canoe trip that made her feel so sad, but she had a sinking feeling that her low mood was linked to Jack.

She liked him too much. She enjoyed being with him too much and she cared far too much about what he thought of her. But such feelings were pointless. Apart from the fact that she belonged to another world and would have to return very soon, there was a remoteness about Jack, an inner sadness and a sense of loss that formed a barrier she could never hope to get past.

She knew nothing about his personal life and he had no wish to share any of it with her. Not even his family name.

She stared at her bare toes, half buried in sand. The problem was that although she accepted these realities with her head, her heart refused to be sensible. She really was becoming a hopeless romantic. Even now, as she watched him standing at the water's edge, alone and apparently unaware of her, she felt an intense yearning that was so painful she wanted to cry.

How crazy!

A loud splash sounded and Jack gave a sudden whoop of triumph as the fishing line strained in his hands.

'You little beauty!' he shouted as he hauled the line in and a large, glistening fish flapped onto the sand at his feet.

She hurried over to him. 'Can we eat it?'

'Too right. This is a golden perch. It'll be delicious.'

'But how can you cook it? We don't have a pan.' She cast a puzzled glance around her at the sandy beach and the simple fire. Jack had mentioned baking. She couldn't imaging baking a whole fish without a kitchen, or at the very least an oven.

Jack's grin was the kind that seemed to reach right inside her. 'I'm going to wrap it in paperbark and cook it bush tucker style. You won't complain when you taste it.'

Fascinated, she watched as he used his pocket knife to cut wide strips of white papery bark from a nearby tree and then fashioned an envelope to hold the fish and the dried onions and carrots that he'd brought from the hut. He bound the parcel with a yam vine he found in the scrub, then looked up at her. His blue eyes flashed as he smiled, and her silly heart did a little gavotte.

By the time he'd finished preparing their meal the coals in his fire had burned down, but he threw some sand onto them to reduce the heat further, then placed the paperbark parcel on top and covered that with another sheet of bark and more sand.

'There's your oven,' he said. 'Now I'll build another fire for warmth and light. The temperature will drop as soon as the sun sets.'

He did this very quickly and efficiently, and in no time they had a bright crackling fire, then he settled his long frame onto the sand beside her.

Having him so close upset the rhythm of Isabella's breathing. She concentrated on a spot on the horizon. The sun had disappeared now, but a fire-like red-gold glow lingered along the distant rim of the hills.

'It's going to be a hot day tomorrow,' Jack said as he watched the sunset. 'It's always like that in the wet season—bearable while it's raining and then hot and steamy afterwards. It gets hotter and hotter until there's another lot of rain.'

'It's very pleasant now,' Isabella suggested. When Jack didn't respond, she added, 'All we need is a pre-dinner G&T or sherry while our dinner cooks.' She wasn't desperate for a drink, but she needed to say something light and frivolous to distract her thoughts from Jack and the astonishing realisation that she would really, really like him to kiss her.

His deep frowning reaction was a surprise. 'I didn't bring any grog on this trip,' he said.

'You don't approve of drinking alcohol?'

'It's not so much that I don't approve, but I tend to give it a miss these days, especially when I'm on my own.' His eyes narrowed as he stared off into the distance. 'I went through a rough patch a couple of years back. There was a time when I lost—someone. Drink and grief can be a bad mix.'

A rash of goosebumps prickled Isabella's arms. Sympathy and surprise formed a lump in her throat. Over the past twenty-four hours she'd become increasingly attuned to Jack's air of sadness. Who had died? Was it a woman he'd loved? A wife?

'I'm very sorry,' she said gently.

He nodded curtly without looking at her and sat very still beside her, staring out past the flickering flames to the river. She could see the tension in his jaw, in the set of his shoulders and the hand fisted on his knee.

Was he already regretting his confession? She switched her attention to the evening star, shimmering brightly against the plush mauve backdrop of the twilight sky. Perhaps he needed to talk...

'Whenever I'm outdoors in the early evening and I'm watching the stars come out I remember my mother,' she said, without looking at him. 'She loved the stars. She knew the names of all the constellations and she would tell me wonderful stories about how they were formed.'

Jack nodded, and his chest rose and fell as he drew in a breath and let it out slowly and deliberately, as if he was willing himself to relax. 'You'll be able to see the Southern Cross soon.'

'Please show it to me. I've always longed to see it.'

Although she wasn't looking at Jack, Isabella was aware that he'd turned to face her.

'You said your mother died, didn't you?'

'Yes,' she said carefully, wondering if he wanted to talk about grief. She kept her gaze ahead, looking out at the water. 'I was only ten, and I was so desperately sad I thought I might never recover.'

'But you did get over it?'

'Eventually, but I'll never stop missing her. She was the most important person in my life. And afterwards...my father didn't seem to know how to talk to me.' Leaning forward to hug her knees, she said, 'Actually, I feel as if I need Mother more than ever now. I have no doubt that she would have helped me stand up to my father against Radik.'

Jack shifted on the sand, moving much closer, and her heart began a hectic dance. His fingers touched her cheek. 'Poor Carmen,' he whispered.

His deep voice was as gentle as the whispering breeze on the water, so tender it stole her breath, so intimate it lit a golden flame low inside her.

'Don't encourage me to feel sorry for myself,' she said with forced brightness.

'How can I distract you?'

Oh, Jack, what a question. You could start by touching your lips to mine.

What was the matter with her? Had she lost all sense of right and wrong? How could she sit here with every cell in her body wanting this man to kiss her when she knew he was deeply troubled by grief?

'Do you want to talk about—your loss, Jack?'

'Not tonight.'

The sudden roughness in his voice made her turn. Shadows and firelight played on his face, showing her tantalising glimpses of the rugged lines of his forehead, nose and cheekbones, the strong beauty of his mouth. 'What do you want to talk about?'

His unsmiling eyes held hers. 'I'm open to suggestions.'

'Well…we'll have to find something to discuss. Otherwise…'

'Otherwise?'

She saw in the flickering light from the fire that he was looking at her with a strange dark hunger. It stirred the heat inside her till her skin felt too tight for her body. 'Otherwise I'll start wishing I really was a gypsy called Carmen.'

'If you were Carmen, what would you do?'

Now? Alone in the wilderness with you, Jack, you impossibly gorgeous man? She tried to laugh, but it came out like a shaky hiccup. 'What do you think Carmen would do?'

He didn't answer.

His gaze held hers and his silence seemed to fill the night. Isabella's heart thudded and the silent sky loomed over them like a purple diamond-studded cave. The scent of sandalwood smoke drifted from the fire, weaving around them like incense.

A burning log snapped and spurted a shower of sparks.

Jack leaned closer.

And Isabella's gasp of surprise was lost inside his kiss. In his wild and wonderful kiss. His mouth was so hot and demanding there was little she could do but cling to his shoulders as he hauled her closer. She couldn't think what was right or wrong; she could only feel herself melting with astonishing speed—surrendering to Jack with trembling willingness. Her lips softened and parted so he could kiss her more deeply, more passionately.

When he pulled back, she made a soft sound of protest.

Their gazes met and held. His intense blue eyes and her midnight-black—sharing amazement at what they'd just done and the surprised certainty that they must do it again.

'Sweet Carmen,' he whispered hoarsely, and he lifted his hand to smooth a strand of hair away from her brow with an exquisitely gentle touch. Her heart fluttered. Lightning flashed through her veins. In a cloud of heat she raised her mouth to meet his.

And this time their parted lips came together with less impatience and more exquisite focus. Jack's hands cradled her face, and gently, slowly, he sipped at her mouth. His hot, hard lips became warm, soft and tantalising, tasting her with deeply sensitive appreciation.

Kissing Jack was different from anything she'd ever known. In the past, the chaste Princess of Amoria had *allowed* herself to be kissed. Now Isabella wanted, no, *needed* to be a full participant.

She wound her arms around his neck, and each time Jack shifted the angle of his mouth to seduce her with the lush, warm slide of his lips and tongue she matched him move for sensual move.

And when he showered her neck and shoulders with a scattering of kisses she arched her head back, to give him access to her needy skin. His fingertips traced pleasure tracks up and down her arms. Each touch made her shivery-hot with desire. She wanted his touch *everywhere*.

She was lost in shocking sensation.

They sank back onto the sand and the full length of their bodies pressed close. Breast to breast, hip to hip, thigh to thigh. Isabella gasped at the force of her reaction.

'Oh, Jack,' she whispered. He felt so strong, so manly, so sexy. Fire and fierce longing spiralled through her.

But he was releasing her again, and this time he swung some distance apart from her. She felt the sudden coolness of the river breeze on her skin instead of his heat. They lay in stunned silence, staring up at the stars, their breathing equally fast and ragged.

'I'm sure I should apologise for that,' he said after some time.

'Please don't.'

She shot a quick glance his way. In the bright velvet moonlight his profile had become a stony mask. She couldn't bear it if he got tense or angry with her. She knew he hadn't planned to kiss her. It had happened spontaneously. Wasn't that the way the best kisses were supposed to happen?

'You wouldn't have apologised to Carmen.'

His smile was thoughtful, then without further comment he sprang to his feet and walked over to the cooking fire, crouched beside it and raked the coals aside with a stick. As he lifted a sheet of bark the delicious aroma of their meal seemed to fill the night air.

How could she think about anything as mundane as eating? It wasn't food she needed. She wanted Jack. She needed him to kiss her again, to hold her. Her body felt hot and hollow; she was burning with need for him.

But his attention was focused strictly on the food.

'That smells wonderful,' she said, forcing enthusiasm into her voice. 'I've just realised I'm starving.'

They ate in silence, balancing their baked fish and vegetables on rough plates fashioned from paperbark, and although she knew that they were both unnerved by the shattering intensity of their kiss, Jack behaved as if it hadn't happened.

'This is absolutely delicious,' she said, but he merely nodded.

After their meal, with the fire banked low and the moon climbing higher, she was surprised to find herself yawning. 'I guess all that paddling must have worn me out,' she said.

'We should get an early night.' His voice was clipped and careful.

Tension arced between them as they crawled into their makeshift tent and lay stiffly side by side in their sleeping bags. They exchanged brief goodnights without touching.

Isabella kept stealing glimpses at the silhouette of Jack's body so close and warm beside her. She knew that he was angry with himself for kissing her. But he *had* kissed her. Of his own accord, he'd kissed her with the kind of mindless passion she'd always dreamed of.

Perhaps she was being foolish, but as she lay there, trying to calm down, trying not to think about snakes or other nasties that might crawl into their tent during the night, she allowed the memory of his hot kiss to settle inside her like a warm and happy promise.

For now it was enough.

Jack lay on his back with his hands stacked under his head, staring out at the triangle of starry sky showing in the inverted V of the tarpaulin.

What a mistake that kiss had been.

He groaned softly. He should have remembered that Isabella had wanted to see the Southern Cross. He should have spent time discussing astronomy instead of kissing the Princess of Amoria as if she was the last woman on earth.

What the hell had he been thinking? A kiss on the hand or the cheek might have been acceptable, but he'd kissed her with a passion that had shaken him to the depths of his being.

And the eagerness of her response had been electrifying—a dynamic blend of sweet, noble girl and sexy, earthy woman. Isabella and Carmen. Had he lost his head? He'd poured his heart and soul into a kiss that he had known was wrong from every perspective.

Apart from the obvious problem that Isabella was blue-blood European royalty and he was a rough-and-ready commoner—an alien from Down Under—he was supposed to be protecting the woman, not using her for his pleasure. And he'd broken a promise to himself too; he was supposed to be dedicating this week to the precious memory of his wife.

But, hell—there was another overriding factor he should have considered. Princess Isabella was young. She was an impressionable romantic and she was running from a rotten cad of a fiancé. The last thing she needed was another cad, a morose, mixed-up recluse, who dallied with her emotions and then abandoned her.

And yet desertion was his only option. When they got to Killymoon he would have to set her ashore and then make himself scarce.

For certain there would be no welcome mat for him at Killymoon homestead.

CHAPTER SIX

A MIST hung over the river when they launched the canoe next morning. It hovered so low they could almost reach up and touch it. The summer morning was deathly still, and as their canoe slipped beneath the white veil there was hardly a sound, except the occasional hush of a rogue breeze stirring the mist-shrouded trees on the bank and the soft plash of their paddles dipping and lifting. Even the birds were quiet.

As the day warmed the mist parted like the curtains in a theatre, drawing open to a beautiful vista of high blue skies, wide brown river and a majestic wall of tall limestone cliffs.

Isabella felt the canoe slow suddenly, and sensed that Jack had braked with a powerful reverse action of his paddle.

'Stop paddling,' came his quiet but authoritative command.

She swung around to look at him, but her motion unsettled the canoe's balance and she heard him mutter harshly under his breath.

Why was he suddenly so tense?

He was staring at the high ridge that towered above the approaching bend in the river, and when she followed his gaze she saw them. Three dark figures on horseback. Standing perfectly still. Watching her and Jack. Fine hairs lifted on the back of her neck.

'Who are they?' she called over her shoulder. 'Is something wrong?'

'Be quiet. Just keep your voice down.'

Alarmed, and hurt by his abrupt tone, she sat very still while he manoeuvred the canoe into the shore, looped a tethering rope around a branch and stepped out onto the bank.

She started to follow him, but he reached out and gripped her roughly by both shoulders.

'Jack? For heaven's sake!'

Without answering he pushed her down so that she landed with an embarrassing jolt onto the seat. What was the matter with him? She'd been trying hard to co-operate. She didn't deserve this rough treatment. With a haughty toss of her head, she glared at him. 'I demand to—'

'This is no time for a royal tantrum,' he said softly through gritted teeth. 'I'll explain everything later, but this is one time you'll just have to take an order. Stay here. Don't on any account get out.'

She sat in stunned silence as Jack strode quickly up the bank. He looked back once, no doubt to check that she was obeying him, and then worked his way up the ridge towards the silent horsemen on the skyline. She could see that they were dark-skinned and dressed in bush shirts and jeans. Their wide-brimmed hats were much like the one Jack had lent her.

As Jack approached them two of the men handed their reins to the third rider, then dismounted and squatted on the ground. They were too far away for her to pick up their voices, but she noted that no one shook hands and that Jack joined them by squatting down on his haunches.

They seemed to be having a serious discussion. Was it her imagination, or was there a ceremonial atmosphere about the meeting?

Stirring uneasily in her seat, she glanced up and down the river, wondering if there were any other silent watchers in the bush. How very little she knew about this wild, remote country—or the man who held her fate in his hands.

The man who'd kissed her with such unexpected passion last night. Was she foolish to have placed so much trust in him?

The meeting didn't take long. Quite soon Jack stood up again and made his way back down the bank. Isabella's gaze lingered on him, watching his easy stride as he wound his way between the trees down the steep slope. Then she switched her attention back to the three mysterious riders.

They were gone.

She was startled. How had they disappeared so quickly? Obviously the men must have mounted their horses and ridden off, but she hadn't sensed any movement. It was hard to squash the feeling that they had simply vanished into the stillness of the bush.

When Jack returned she jumped up eagerly, anxious to join him on the bank.

'No, Isabella,' he said quickly. 'Stay in the canoe. I'll tell you what this is all about, but don't step onto the land.' At least his voice was softer, gentler, and she sensed an underlying plea for her to obey.

Puzzled, she sat quietly and waited as he squatted down, reached into the river with one hand and splashed water onto his face.

Then he spoke quietly. 'Those men are Wondarra, and this section of the river—the bend and the ridge—is sacred to them.'

'Are they Aborigines?'

'Yes.'

'I had no idea there were other people out here. I thought you said the Kingsley-Lairds owned this country?'

'They do, in legal terms, but the Wondarra people are the traditional owners of this land. They've been here for many thousands of years and they have special right of access to sacred sites. We have to respect that.'

'I see, but why were you so tense?' *So rude to me,* she almost added, but thought better of it.

'I guess you're used to giving orders, Isabella, but so am I.' Jack sighed. 'In some ways I shouldn't be telling you this, but that ridge and the riverbank here are what they call men's business. As far as the Wondarra are concerned, it's no place for a woman. Even the sound of a woman's voice can be offensive. I had to go and pay my respects and quietly assure those men that there would be no problem with you.'

'Good heavens.' She digested the information. She didn't like it, but now didn't seem an appropriate moment to become a rampant feminist. And she couldn't help feeling grateful that Jack was her guide and understood the territory. If she'd stumbled on those men on her own she would have been terrified. 'So everything is OK now?'

'Sure—just keep quiet and do exactly what I say for the next twenty kilometres.'

'Twenty kilometres? You're joking, aren't you?'

He laughed. 'Of course. But it was worth a try, Your Highness.'

By the time they stopped for a swim Isabella was so hot and tired she didn't hesitate to join Jack in the water. And although there were slimy river weeds, that he knew must have touched her on the leg or wrapped around her ankle, she bravely refused to scream. In fact she didn't show any sign of fear.

After lunch they rested, sprawling on their backs in the shade of a wattle tree where the filtered sunlight played on their closed eyelids.

'Don't let me go to sleep,' Isabella said. 'I might never want to wake up.'

'You want to talk?' Jack asked lazily with his eyes still closed.

'If it will keep me awake.'

'Tell me a little more about this fiancé of yours.'

'What would you like to know?'

'You've told me he's dashing and charming. Does that mean you were ever in love with him?'

She didn't answer.

Jack opened his eyes and turned his head towards her. Dappled sunlight stencilled patterns on her face, but he could see the tension in the tightening of her mouth. 'Isabella?'

'Let me put it this way,' she said quietly, without looking at him. 'Radik—'

Jack rolled quickly onto his side to face her. She looked so suddenly distressed he had to butt in. 'He wasn't hurting you, was he?'

'He didn't hurt me physically, but he frightened me.' She swallowed, but kept her gaze strictly on the overhead tree branch. 'I'd been worried for some time about my chances for future happiness. We're nothing alike. Radik likes fast cars and all-night parties and champagne by the bucketload. Cannes is his favourite watering hole.'

'And what about you? What do you like?'

'I like simple things.' As she turned his way she smiled, and her right cheek dimpled.

'Define simple.'

'Oh, going for long walks in the countryside in the late afternoon, when there's a lovely soft glow over everything. Growing my own flowers and baking cakes.'

Jack laughed. 'You should have been a farmer's wife.'

Isabella's smile faded. 'Being born a princess is an accident. It's not necessarily a privilege.'

'Are you saying that you wish you hadn't been born into royalty?'

She frowned and sighed. 'Actually, I'd rather not talk about it. It'll spoil this lovely day.'

'But are you unhappy with your life?'

'Not unhappy, exactly...but... Oh, I don't know. Since my mother died my father's become more remote and pigheaded—' She broke off and sent him a grimace, as if she felt guilty for betraying the King, but then she added, 'My father's main form of communication these days is to send me orders to attend a formal function or to receive certain guests.'

'Or to marry the Count of Montez?'

'It's very nearly as bad as that.'

'Well—I know all about pigheaded fathers.'

'Do you?' She sat up quickly. 'Will you tell me? Come on, it's only fair, when I've told you so much about me.'

It was damn tempting to tell her. After all, she was a stranger and she wouldn't be gossiping in his social set. But once started he might find himself telling her too much. Everything. 'Not now,' he said.

'Why are you so secretive?'

He sighed. 'There's no need to discuss my life. You have enough problems for both of us.'

Isabella's disappointment showed in her eyes and the drooping set of her mouth. But then she shrugged and looked off into the distance. 'You're right when you say I'd probably make a good farmer's wife. Sometimes I think I should have been born a peasant.'

'Or a gypsy?'

'Yes.' Her eyes met his again. She smiled and her eyes shone and the dimple returned. 'Or a gypsy.'

He felt a sudden catch in his breathing. It had been damn stupid of him to start mentioning gypsies after the trouble talk of Carmen had led to last night.

'Actually, I do have a link to gypsies,' Isabella said.

'In what way?' he asked cautiously.

'Well—according to my nanny, a gypsy woman came into the palace on the night I was born and announced a prophecy.'

'About you?'

'Yes. She said predictable stuff about the baby princess growing up to be beautiful—'

'Well, she got that wrong,' Jack interrupted.

Isabella poked her pink tongue at him and tossed a twig onto his face.

'That's not the interesting bit,' she retorted. 'She said that the princess would have the heart of a gypsy. And you know—I'd forgotten about that until you asked me the other night if I was a gypsy.'

Jack tried to ignore the jolt in his stomach as he stared at her. 'But you don't believe it, do you?'

'I don't know,' she murmured softly. 'I don't suppose so. But the other thing she said is kind of interesting too.'

'What's that?' He might as well ask. She would tell him anyway. But suddenly Jack wished they weren't having this conversation.

To his surprise Isabella looked embarrassed. She bit her lower lip, then sent him a guilty smile and shrugged. 'She said that I would only find lasting happiness in a distant land— a land where the cross hangs in the midnight sky.'

Another jolt flashed through Jack. He leapt to his feet. He'd heard *enough*. 'I suppose you believe messages in tealeaves in the bottom of a teacup, too?'

'You think it's nonsense?' She scrambled to her feet and stood looking at him with a complicated smile that managed to be both defensive and challenging at once.

'Yes, Isabella. I think it's a very pretty romantic story, but it's nonsense.' Without looking at her again, he strode back to the canoe. 'Let's get going.'

*　　*　　*

When they eventually pulled up at the end of the long day, they headed straight back into the water for another swim. Floating on their backs, they watched the clouds turn pink and gold as the cool water soothed their tired muscles.

And as their meal cooked they sprawled drowsily on the bank, keeping their hunger at bay by munching on dried apple rings.

Jack was determined not to make the same mistake as last night. One kiss was an error of judgement; a second would be an idiotic disaster. He hunted for practical things to discuss—something that had nothing to do with gypsies…

'Have you sent any messages back home since you left?' he asked.

Isabella flopped onto her stomach so she could look at him while she spoke. The casual movement was unexpectedly graceful. But then everything she did was graceful. All day he'd been sitting behind her, watching her paddle the canoe, and the smooth glide and lift of her shoulderblades and arms had been damn captivating.

'I rang a girlfriend from Darwin airport,' she told him. 'I didn't tell her where I was. I just asked her to let my father know I'm safe and well.'

She frowned and threaded her last ring of dried apple onto her little finger and stared at it. 'The first thing I should do when we get to Killymoon homestead is make a phone call home. I never meant to disappear quite so completely.'

'You'll have to be careful,' Jack said. 'Your fiancé will probably have people waiting for your call so they can trace it.'

She sighed. 'Yes. I guess the palace will be overrun with detectives by now. I'll have to think of someone outside the palace to ring— perhaps one of the nurses at the hospital.'

Settling onto his side, he dug a bent elbow into the sand and propped his head on one hand. 'Tell me some more about this hospital work you do.'

Isabella's eyes signalled mild surprise and she shrugged. 'I started it in my teens because I wanted to carry on where my mother left off. Mother was greatly loved by our people. She was deeply committed to her charity work—especially with the homeless and the dying.' She smiled wistfully. 'For me, quiet behind-the-scenes work seems to make up for all the razzle-dazzle.'

'Of being a public figure?'

'Yes.'

'The dignity of service?'

She shot him a sharp look, as if she feared he might be making fun of her.

'It's deeply satisfying and a privilege to have the opportunity to serve people,' she said defensively. 'I find it incredibly rewarding.'

'What's the most rewarding thing you've done?'

She didn't hesitate. 'When I've spent time with people who are dying alone—people with no family around them. You'd be surprised—even in a tiny country like Amoria there are too many people brought in from off the streets. I like to be there for them, to show them that at least one person cares.'

Jack's jaw dropped as he stared at her. He was sideswiped by a mental picture of this vibrant, young and beautiful girl caring for a dying vagrant. 'That—that's quite something.'

'No matter who a person is, everyone deserves to depart this life supported by an atmosphere of serenity and respect. And love.'

Jack's thoughts flew to Geri, and a welling of pain dammed his throat and stabbed at the backs of his eyes. He swiped a hand over his face.

'I'm sorry, Jack,' Isabella said quickly, her eyes growing luminous with sudden sympathy. 'You probably don't want to talk about this.'

'No,' he insisted. 'It's—it's very interesting. How do you go about establishing this atmosphere of—of serenity?'

She sat up and leant forward, wrapping her arms around her knees. For a thoughtful moment she looked away, watching the flight of a black and white ibis, then she tipped her head to one side and looked back at him with such tender concern that his throat grew tight and painful.

'It depends on the circumstances,' she said. 'Many times it's simply a case of being there and being a calm presence. Holding a hand. Touch can be very reassuring. Some of these people have lived for years without any human contact.'

To his dismay, a strangled gasp broke from his throat. There'd been no comforting hand at the end for his wife. No gentle, peaceful release. Everything about her death had been so unfair.

'Jack?'

He heard Isabella's soft voice, but he couldn't see her. His eyes were awash.

'Talking about this is upsetting you,' she said.

He closed his eyes and tried to blink them clear. Tried *not* to remember. But the memories forced themselves upon him.

He was back in that dreadful delivery room. Geri was pale and exhausted from her long and difficult labour. And a grim-faced doctor was telling them the harrowing news that their daughter had been stillborn.

Then, while their shock was still at its sharpest and most searing, he was listening in horror as the hospital staff became agitated again and began to talk about a dangerous haemorrhage. Next minute they were rushing Geri away from him to the operating theatre.

He'd hurried after her as they'd dashed her down the long hospital corridor. He'd never forget how alive her red hair had looked, like a startling bright flame against the white pillow. Poor Geri. She'd been so terrified. She'd reached her hand back to him.

He'd touched his hand to hers briefly and then she had gone, where he couldn't follow, disappearing through the swing doors of the operating theatre.

And, God help him, she'd never come back.

'I wasn't there for her,' he said, his voice cracking under the awful weight of his sadness. 'I wasn't there for Geri.'

'Geri?' Isabella whispered.

'My wife.'

'Oh, Jack, I'm so sorry.'

Swinging into a sitting position, he stared blindly at the ground between his feet. 'She died in childbirth. The baby died too.'

Isabella's cry sounded as filled with pain as the weight in his chest.

'I wasn't with her when she died. They took her away and they wouldn't let me go with her.' He was trembling now, shaking with the effort to hold back the force of his emotions. 'I didn't know she wouldn't come back. I refused to believe I might be saying goodbye. I—I didn't even tell her I loved her.'

Suddenly he couldn't help it. He was weeping. Weeping harder than he had in three years. The grief he'd fought so hard to bury claimed him now, and his tears came in painful chunks, like pieces of debris being chipped away from a fossil.

He had no idea when Isabella moved, but he could feel her behind him, her hands on his shaking shoulders and her cheek pressed against the back of his neck, her hands stroking up and down his arms.

'Jack, poor Jack,' she murmured softly, and she looped her arms around him and hugged him. With his back against her, she rocked him gently, silently. And he couldn't stop crying. There was nothing he could do but give in to the racking sobs.

For three years now he'd been carefully hoarding his grief, warding off sympathy, keeping well-meaning friends at a distance. Now he felt as if Isabella had cracked open the hard protective shell he'd drawn around himself.

And it felt perplexingly right to turn into her warm arms, for her to hold him with his head pressed against her shoulder. For her to thread her fingers into the hair at the back of his head and to rub his scalp with a slow, soothing touch.

When at last he managed to get his emotions under control and grow calmer again, he lifted his face and took a huge deep breath. Without a word, she released him from the hug.

She moved to sit beside him once more.

'You mustn't be too hard on yourself,' she said gently. 'It's terrible when there's a sudden emergency. There's so little you can do. You aren't given a chance to say goodbye.'

He wiped his face on his sleeve and looked out at the river, where the moonlit water raced and splashed over a rocky shelf of rock. Isabella remained silent, but her words kept echoing in his head.

You aren't given a chance to say goodbye.

That was the worst of it. He'd been so numb with shock that afterwards, when they'd taken him to see Geri, he'd just stood there in frozen disbelief.

He'd never said goodbye. Not then, nor in the years to follow.

For three years he'd resisted letting Geri go. First he'd drowned himself in drink, and then he'd buried himself in his work—and throughout it all he'd cut himself off from friends and family. He'd been so angry he'd locked himself away, but none of his defences had helped. For three years he'd been living in a half-dead limbo.

Even this week he'd planned at Pelican's End had been an escape from the reality that Geri was gone. He'd been planning to recreate the times they'd spent there together. But perhaps he should have been finding a way to say farewell.

Lost in these thoughts, he was dimly aware that beside him Isabella was standing and walking over to the fire.

'I think our dinner might be ready,' she said.

He sniffed the air and leapt to his feet. 'Struth, it's sure to be done.' He hurried to join her and raked back the coals. 'Just as well you spoke up, or we'd probably be going hungry tonight.'

As it was, their fish was cooked to perfection, but Jack was lost in his thoughts and Isabella was exhausted from her long day on the river. Her eyelids began to droop even before she'd finished her meal.

'I don't think I can stay awake a moment longer,' she said.

'Off to bed with you.' Jack chanced a light kiss on her cheek. 'Goodnight.' As she began to walk away he added, 'And thanks.'

He knew he didn't have to explain what he was thanking her for.

She smiled. 'Goodnight, Jack.' Somewhere in the distance dingoes howled, and she shot a nervous glance to their swags lying in the dark, out of range of the fire's light. 'I still don't enjoy being out in the bush at night. You won't be too far away, will you?'

'I'll be right here,' he told her.

I just need a little time…

Rolling a log over to the fire, he sat there, staring into the mesmerising flames. He needed time to sit and to think about Geri…

And to remember their tiny daughter, Annie—the poor little sweetheart with her cap of fine red hair—who'd never received the gift of life.

For ages he sat there, staring at the red and orange glow, replaying memories.

After Geri's death, despite his rebuffs, well-meaning folk had tried to explain the unexplainable in clichés, and he'd dismissed their suggestions rudely. But tonight those few words of Isabella's had made sense… He didn't get to say goodbye…

Somehow tonight, out here beneath a million watching stars, the simple fact of Geri's death seemed so much more believable. It was as simple a truth as this river flowing beside him, always moving onwards towards the sea. Like the river, his own life was irreversible. He couldn't go back. He couldn't recapture his life with Geri.

He rose stiffly and dragged another thick piece of timber onto the fire. He watched the blue tongues of flame lick around it, growing bolder and redder. For three years he hadn't been living—he'd been merely surviving.

And yet surely if he'd learnt anything from this tragedy he had to recognise that life was a gift. What was he doing with his? Wasting it?

Throwing back his head, he let out a deep sigh as he stared up at the vast sky, resplendent with its lavish expanse of fiery stars. There was a lot to think about.

*   *   *

Isabella woke just before dawn.

The world was still shadowed and very quiet, although she could hear the sounds of the bush—a bird warbling, the soft ripple of the river running over rocks, the muffled lowing of cattle and the clomping of their hooves somewhere in the distance.

Overhead, a chink of sky between the treetops shimmered with the first pale glow of morning.

Soon it would be daylight.

And today they would reach Killymoon.

By Jack's calculations she'd be with the Kingsley-Lairds by lunchtime, which meant her time alone with him was almost over.

She turned her head so she could look at him as he lay beside her. The pearly pre-dawn light spilled through the treetops and slid under the tarpaulin to etch his profile with a watery sheen. On impulse, she propped herself up on one elbow to improve the angle of her view.

Now she could see his rough curls and his strong brow, the thick stubby brushes of his eyelashes, the jut of his nose and the shadow in the little V-shaped valley that ran between his nose and his lips.

His lips!

Oh, mercy. A terrible thrill darted straight to her loins. The other night those lips had ravished hers. They'd swept her away to a sensuous world she'd only dared visit in her dreams. A world of reckless urgency. Delicate surrender.

She would have surrendered. If Jack hadn't stopped kissing her she probably would have gone the whole way with him—had *sex* with him. She, a king's daughter, had almost made love to a man who hadn't even told her his full name.

Even now, despite what he'd told her about his wife, the very thought of Jack making love to her made her burn. She couldn't get the thought out of her head.

No man had ever made her feel so restless and aroused. Never. Certainly not Radik— even though she'd thought she loved him enough to marry him. How strange that it should happen now.

Perhaps she was turning into Carmen. Out here in the Outback—where she had no possessions except one set of clothes, where she bathed in rock pools and used acacia seed pods for soap, where she let her hair go wild and her skin grow tanned—she felt as if she was throwing off a lifetime of restraints.

Losing sight of Princess Isabella?

Heavens, just thinking about how different she felt now made her want to reach out to touch Jack. Her fingers curled impatiently. She could imagine the sleep-warm heat of his skin, the alien roughness of his unshaved jaw, the supple strength of his arms, the springy hair on his bare chest... Oh, help! What about the rest of him? How would *that* feel?

A wave of longing rolled upwards through her, stealing her breath, making her shiver and tremble. Outside the mantle of darkness was fading. It would soon be morning. Jack would wake and jump out of bed. He'd spring into action, busying himself with the tasks of breaking camp.

But she wanted him to stay here beside her...

What would Carmen do if she wanted a man? Wanted him to hold her one more time?

Would she kiss him awake?

Isabella leaned closer.

He looked almost boyish as he lay asleep. His lips were soft and relaxed now. The other night they'd been fierce and demanding. Could she make them come alive again? Oh, dear heaven, dared she?

Would he be angry with her?

A slight dip of her head was all it would take.

Her breathing grew fast and shallow and her heart raced as she leaned closer, then lowered her face...

Her hair brushed his cheek.

His eyes snapped open.

'Isabella.' In a flash his arms gripped her shoulders, holding her in position, mere inches above him.

'Good morning,' she murmured.

'Morning.' His blue eyes were instantly alert and puzzled.

'I was just—um—checking to see if you were awake.'

He looked over her shoulder to the dawn shadows and lifted one eyebrow. 'So early?'

She gave a shy, twisted smile. 'I was feeling—restless.'

'Restless, Isabella?'

'Yes, very—restless.'

Jack shot another quick glance outside and Isabella felt a punch of dismay. Any second now he was going to become all sensible and businesslike. He would push her aside as easily as he would a sapling branch that blocked his path and jump up and start lighting the fire for breakfast.

She took a deep breath. 'I'm feeling a *Carmen* kind of restless.'

The puzzled wariness in Jack's eyes intensified.

For a long, long moment he held her inches from him. His Adam's apple worked in his throat as he stared hard, as if he needed to be very clear that he'd understood her message.

Then the steely coolness in his gaze melted. His mouth tilted. 'Are you coming on to me, Carmen?'

'Coming on?' She'd never heard the term before, but she was almost certain she knew what it meant.

A dark tinge crept up his neck and along his cheekbones. His eyes were glazed with heat. 'You know what will happen if we start kissing again?'

'Um.' She swallowed nervously. 'Yes. I think I do.'

'Shouldn't you be exercising some royal caution, Your Highness?'

'*No!* No, Jack.' Her impatience was *so* embarrassing. But she was trembling with the need to feel his kiss, his touch.

'No?'

She shook her head.

His eyes burned her as he watched the movement of her hair. He continued to hold her suspended above him while he let his smouldering gaze travel slowly, slowly downwards, to take in the rest of her. Touching her everywhere with his eyes.

Suddenly self-conscious, she remembered that she'd slept in one of his old grey T-shirts. Perhaps he thought she looked a fright? Then she saw the scorching heat in his eyes. Perhaps not…

'Come here,' he whispered, pulling her down to him.

CHAPTER SEVEN

WITH excruciating slowness his hands caressed her skin. He kissed her lower lip, then drew it between his teeth and took a teasing, lazy nibble. The tug of his mouth and the silken touch of his fingers caused a sweet ache low inside her. She closed her eyes.

'You're a very interesting woman,' he murmured as he nuzzled her neck just below her ear. 'A man never knows what to expect.'

'And yet I know exactly what to expect from you.' She managed to sound a million times braver than she felt.

'Oh, yes? And what might that be?'

'Perfection.'

He chuckled lazily and tucked a strand of her hair behind her ear, then nipped her earlobe and traced the edge of her jaw with his tongue. Ripples of pleasure shivered over and under her skin.

'Talk about high expectations.'

She knew he was secretly pleased.

His lips found her mouth again, and his kiss was hot and sleepy as his hands slid slowly down her arms, then found her hips and the hem of her T-shirt. His fingers toyed with the flimsy cotton, then ducked underneath to trace sensuous circles on her bare lower back and her buttocks.

Her mind almost melted. Already just having him touch her this way was driving her wild. How would she cope when he got to— to details?

She felt a brief moment of panic.

But then she told herself that this wasn't the moment to be afraid. This was what she'd been dreaming about ever since she'd met Jack. If he sensed her fear he might suspect her secret, and she couldn't bear for him to turn away from her now. She'd started this. She had to think and act like Carmen.

Hoping he couldn't see that her hands were shaking, she eased back from him and lifted the T-shirt.

'Oh, my...'

Jack's breath caught and he lost all hope of finding the words to remind Isabella again that this was dangerous. He couldn't even tell her how lovely she was.

The first light of morning crept through the bush, reaching into their tent to touch her skin with a creamy glow, and he wanted to tell her how perfect she was, how very sweet and lush her rosy-tipped breasts, how graceful the curve from her waist to her hip. But his throat constricted on an upsurge of need.

He could only hope that the touch of his hands and lips and body would speak for him.

But easy, man, he warned himself. Take it easy.

Their makeshift tent became their world.

They were two warm bodies coming together in a sweet and tender pact. Their thighs entwined. His palms cupped her breasts and she was adrift on a sea of sensations.

She couldn't hold back her soft sighs of pleasure. Beneath the caressing pressure of his hands and his mouth her skin grew warmer and tighter, her limbs heavy with desire. He was so good to her, touching and kissing and tasting every part of her that longed for and needed his loving.

Why had it taken her twenty-five years to discover how impossibly beautiful lovemaking could be?

All sense of panic faded. Instead there was music building inside her. Grand music. Growing stronger, louder, more passionate, pulling her with it, tighter and higher.

From a long way off she thought she heard Jack's voice, whispering how desirable and sexy she was. But it was he who was sexy. He had made her this way. He'd turned her into this sensuous, exultant woman of fire.

And then, too soon, she was falling. But, oh, what a splendid, glorious, trembling fall it was.

'Jack. Oh, Jack.'

His heart drummed as she whispered his name over and over, as she clung to him and kissed him, trailed her soft lips over his jaw.

And he was rocketing out of control. This woman, who had been firing his blood for days now, had lured him to the point of no return. Hot need pulsed through him as he settled her slim hips beneath him.

She smiled up at him and her dark eyes reflected his heat. For a heartbeat he thought he also saw a flash of fear, but she was whispering his name again, wrapping her soft arms and silken legs around him, and he gave up the bitter battle with his conscience as she welcomed him into her sweet warmth.

Shortly before noon their canoe shot around a sharp bend in the river.

'There's Killymoon,' Jack said.

Isabella's stomach took an unexpected dive as she looked ahead at what might almost have been a mirage. A lush green sweep of carefully groomed lawn cut a wide swathe through the smoky grey-green tangle of bush. The lawn formed an emerald-green velvet curve from the riverbank to the top of a rise. On the crest of the slope a long, low house reclined with graceful ease beneath tall, spreading shade trees.

'There you have it—the complete pastoral symphony,' Jack commented dryly.

She squinted beneath her broad-brimmed hat, trying to make out details. The house looked rather grand for an Outback farmhouse. It seemed to be fronted by shaded verandahs with slender white columns. She thought she could make out panelled French doors with timber frames, deep blue storm shutters and large planter tubs spilling with a blaze of bright crimson and white flowers, possibly bougainvillaea.

After days of nothing but wilderness it was a shock to come across such classic signs of civilisation.

Here there would be hot baths and shampoo, comfy beds and clean sheets, milk and fresh fruit and brewed coffee.

'It looks lovely,' she said, turning back to Jack, but her heart stumbled when she saw the grim expression on his face.

All morning he'd been unnaturally quiet and withdrawn. Ever since…

What's the matter, Jack? She couldn't voice the question, but it echoed in her head. Was he thinking, as she was, that once they reached Killymoon there would be no more opportunities for stolen kisses—for making love?

'Let's pull over for a moment,' he said, and immediately matched his actions to his words by dipping his paddle deeply into the water and steering them towards the river's edge.

They slipped the canoe close to a shelf of sandy bank, hidden from the house by a pocket of thick scrub. Jack moored their craft by looping a hank of rope around a broken stump, then jumped ashore. He offered her his hand and the canoe rocked gently in the shallow water as she stepped out of it onto the bank.

She shivered and tried to shrug off a shadowy feeling of darkness, a kind of premonition of deep sadness. How could sadness follow so quickly on the heels of the intense happiness she'd experienced in Jack's arms?

He'd lit an astonishing fire in her. All she'd been able to think of since was how much she desired him. And it didn't feel wrong to want him so fiercely. Loving him had been like opening herself to goodness, embracing a perfect truth.

It didn't make sense that she should feel so low now.

Was her mood a reflection of the bleakness in his eyes?

'What is it, Jack? What's the matter?'

He stared at the ground between his feet. 'This is as far as I can take you. It's time to say goodbye.'

The sandy bank seemed to crumble beneath her. 'But you're coming up to the homestead with me, aren't you? Don't you want to speak to the Kingsley-Lairds?'

'No.'

No? How could he want to leave her so soon? 'Why—why not?'

His jaw squared as he avoided her despairing eyes and looked out across the river. 'I have good reasons, but I don't want to expand on them now. Don't ask me to, Isabella.'

Oh, God. Why hadn't she thought this through? They'd never discussed it, but she'd assumed that Jack would stay with her. Somehow she'd kidded herself that her champion would stick by her side till the bitter end. How foolish. That only happened in Hollywood.

Wake up to the real world, Isabella.

'I've never pushed you to tell me anything about yourself, Jack. I guess it's too late now.'

'I guess it is.' He sighed loudly and finally brought his gaze back to meet hers. His eyes were hard, like blue marble. 'Just trust me when I say this is best,' he said. 'I'll hang around to make sure you're OK. If you don't come back in half an hour I'll assume everything is fine. Then I'll head back up the river.'

A shaft of pain strafed through her like a bullet. She wouldn't see Jack again.

It didn't seem possible that this was it. The end. 'It's such a long way for you to go, right back to Pelican's End on your own. You'll be working against the current.'

'Don't worry about me. I'll be all right.'

But I won't be all right, Jack. She couldn't pretend to be cool about his sudden desertion.

Reaching up, she removed his akubra hat from her head and set it carefully on top of the tree stump that moored the canoe. With the hat gone, her hair tumbled down past her shoulders and she saw him flinch. His eyes became dark, brooding storm clouds as he looked at her.

'I wasn't expecting to have to say goodbye so soon,' she said.

He shrugged. 'Sooner or later. It doesn't make a lot of difference.'

'I—I don't know how to begin to start saying thank you. And—and I have absolutely no idea how to say goodbye.'

He forced a weak grin. 'It's only a matter of one little word.'

'How can you be so flippant?'

'Because there's no point in being serious.' After a beat he added, 'Not about us.'

She felt so suddenly ill that she swayed and almost fell into the river. Jack's hand whipped out to steady her and she inhaled sharply when he touched her.

For breathless seconds they stood poised on the edge of the riverbank. His hand at her elbow.

'Isabella, why didn't you tell me?'

'Tell you? What are you talking about?'

'You know.'

Yes, she did. If possible, she felt even more wretched. She opened her mouth, but she couldn't speak.

'I'm talking about this morning. Don't you think you should have told me you were a virgin?'

Her hand clutched her throat. He was angry with her. He'd been angry with her ever since… She shot him one distressed, desperate glance, then swung abruptly away.

But Jack caught her arm again. 'It's a fair question,' he said more gently. 'Why didn't you tell me?'

Because I wanted you, Jack. Because I think I love you and I don't think I'll ever get over you. I don't think I could ever feel the same about another man.

Her insides were collapsing.

She might have died on the spot from mortification if her years of palace discipline hadn't come to her aid. Gathering her dignity, she squared her shoulders and lifted her chin. 'I was afraid you would reject me if you knew.'

Jack sighed and rubbed a hand over his brow. 'Heck, Isabella, a princess's virginity isn't something to be taken lightly. You shouldn't have thrown it away on a chance stranger. A bloke you hardly know.'

Oh, Jack! She whipped her head to the side so he couldn't see the rush of tears. 'I didn't offer myself lightly,' she said in a small, choked voice.

He groaned. 'Maybe I phrased that badly.' He took a step towards her. 'I'm sorry, Isabella.'

'I'm not sorry, Jack.' This time when she turned back to him she did so without bothering to wipe her eyes. 'I'm twenty-five years old and I don't consider that I've squandered myself. I wanted you, Jack. I claimed the same right that every other woman has. I made a choice for myself.'

Suddenly he was reaching for her, pulling her against him, clasping her tightly to his heaving chest. He pressed his warm lips to her damp cheek, lifted her hair to kiss the curve of her neck.

'You are one very special woman,' he murmured huskily. 'I just need you to understand that what we shared can't lead anywhere. You do know that, don't you? We belong to different worlds.'

She couldn't help herself. His touch made her hollow and shivery. Aching with need for him. She wound her arms around his neck and pressed her body into his and kissed him full on the mouth. His answering kiss was as impassioned and urgent as hers. He tasted of sunshine and the salt of her tears.

He groaned softly, hauling her harder against him. His arms imprisoned her in an embrace that stole her breath, but then, too soon, he tore his mouth from hers.

'Tell me you understand, Isabella.'

'I don't want to understand.'

'You must.'

With a miserable sigh, she loosened the circle of her arms. 'The only thing I understand for sure is that I've never felt about any other man the way I feel about you.'

'Oh, God. You'll get over this.' His voice was choked and hoarse. 'You'll go back to your world, where you belong, and you'll clear up this current problem and ditch your fiancé. And for sure there'll be some perfect prince waiting for you in the wings.'

She used the backs of her hands to wipe her eyes. 'That's a fairy tale, Jack.'

'No!' he cried, and he flung his arms wide to take in the river, the canoe, the bush. '*This* is the fairy tale. You'll see that when you get back home. To the *real* world.' He gave her shoulder an encouraging squeeze. 'The important thing is to keep your head. Be very careful. Make sure John Kingsley-Laird understands how serious your situation is and that you need to lie low until after Saturday.'

The conviction in his voice and the hard practicality of his advice sapped the last shreds of her hope. Jack really meant it. Their time together was over. In spite of her despair she felt a bleak resignation settle over her. This was it. She was on her own again.

Wiping her face on her sleeve, she drew in a deep, sad breath.

'Now go,' he said, giving her a gentle push.

Looking over her shoulder to the right, she saw a narrow track winding through the tangle of scrub. Then she turned back to him and the ferocious blaze in his eyes almost broke her heart.

She tried to smile.

He nodded grimly. 'Good luck.'

Quite sure that her heart was breaking, she slowly began to walk away from him.

CHAPTER EIGHT

A DOG came bounding towards Isabella as she emerged onto the lawn in front of Killymoon homestead. Tail wagging madly, the young golden Labrador sniffed at her legs and circled around her, leaping with doggy excitement.

'Hello, boy.' She gave him a tentative pat and he pranced beside her as she continued up the sloping lawn towards the homestead. As she neared it, a woman came out of the house and stood at the top of the wide stone steps. She shaded her eyes with a raised hand as she watched Isabella's approach.

Framed by her rambling, beautiful home, and dressed in pristine white trousers with a crisp blue and white striped cotton shirt, she looked the epitome of country charm. Her straight silver hair was held back from her classically handsome face by a black velvet band, and she carried a flat cane basket and secateurs as if she'd been planning a little light gardening.

'Buster, come here, boy,' she called to the dog as she watched Isabella's approach.

'Hello, Elizabeth,' Isabella said as she reached the bottom step.

Elizabeth Kingsley-Laird's mouth dropped open. 'It's not— It can't be—'

'I'm afraid it can be, and it is.'

'Princess Isabella?'

As she climbed the steps Isabella lifted the heavy tangle of curls away from her face. 'I'm not surprised that you had trouble recognising me. I'm sorry to arrive unannounced.'

'My dear, for heaven's sake, don't apologise,' Elizabeth cried. 'I'm just so surprised. Good heavens. You're getting married on Saturday. We're all packed to fly off to your wedding.' She flashed a worried glance towards the river. 'Where have you come from?'

Isabella told her briefly about driving her car into the flooded creek.

'Good heavens, dear. Pelican's End is so far away. How on earth did you get here?'

'By canoe.'

'Canoe?' Elizabeth's jaw dropped.

'It's a long story.'

'I'm sure it must be.' Hastily setting the basket on the ground, she held out her arms to Isabella. 'You poor girl. I mustn't keep you standing out in the heat. Come inside. John's out with the vet today, making some last-minute checks on his prize bulls, but he'll be home later this evening. What a surprise he'll get.'

Walking into Killymoon's sitting room was like entering the private rooms in the Valdenza Palace. Walls in a soft shade of yellow, generous couches, vases of fresh flowers and floors covered by antique rugs created a feeling of refined elegance overlaid by a comfortable and welcoming warmth.

But as Isabella glanced around at the beautiful landscapes on the walls, the display cabinet of antique porcelain and the collection of silver-framed photographs on the table by the window, she felt strangely uneasy to be surrounded by creature comforts.

She glanced down at her broken fingernails, her scratched legs, muddy shoes and crumpled clothes, and grinned ruefully. She felt as if she'd been living on the river and camping out in the wilderness for months rather than days.

'Let me guess,' said Elizabeth. 'A cup of tea or coffee first and then a long soak in a bubble bath?'

'That sounds like heaven.'

'And then you can tell me your story.'

Jack paddled like a man possessed, hoping against hope that the physical discomfort of pitting his muscles against a strong current might sidetrack him from thinking about Isabella.

It was a vain hope. While every dip of his paddle took him physically further from her, his thoughts held her plum at the centre of his focus.

He couldn't get rid of the memory of the tears in her beautiful dark eyes. They'd shimmered like brave stars when she'd said good-bye. He'd done that to her. She was already in trouble, running for her life from a cad of a fiancé, and he'd caused her more pain.

He cursed himself for his weakness. He should have resisted her. But three years of hard work and anger could only provide a man with limited immunity. He was bound to be susceptible to the appeal of a gutsy, beautiful woman.

But *this* woman? God help him, he'd deflowered a virgin princess! Surely that had to be a sin in any man's language.

Isabella had trusted him to be her knight in shining armour and he'd violated that trust. And the fact that she'd given herself so freely and tenderly didn't make him feel any better.

It was crazy. The last thing, the very *last thing* that should have happened this week was for him to make love to an exotic and attractive stranger. But she was so damn lovely, so warm and lush and willing, and just thinking about her brought a pain to his throat as if he'd swallowed broken glass.

It should have been a cinch to send her packing off to Killymoon, but as she'd walked away from him in her rumpled white shirt, with her dark hair falling past her shoulders, she'd looked so damn beautiful he'd almost called out. *Carmen*. Just in time he'd bitten back on the cry.

And the very minute she'd gone he'd started to worry. All the reasoning that had seemed like common sense before—the assumption that she would be perfectly safe—made no sense at all now.

She'd trusted *him* and she'd expected that he, Jack, would stick with her till all danger was past.

He'd damn well let her down.

And he'd lost his peace of mind.

That was the dilemma, he realised grimly. Isabella had come to mean more to him than he cared to admit. When he'd watched her walk away from him into the bush he'd been hit by the thought that he might be losing his best chance of regaining his life.

But that was crazy.

How could he share his life with a European princess?

Who was lost in a dumb fairy tale now?

Any way he looked at this it felt bad—a no-win situation. Which was why he kept paddling. And feeling bad.

It was mid-afternoon when Isabella saw the photograph.

She and a shocked Elizabeth were in the sitting room, after an exhaustive discussion of her news about Radik, when her attention was caught by the collection of photographs on a nearby table.

'I must take a closer look at your family,' she said, conscious that she'd been talking about herself for too long.

'By all means,' Elizabeth agreed.

The silver-framed photos ranged from old sepia portraits of solemn-looking ancestors in the Victorian era to more recent wedding photos, holiday shots and chubby babies—and towards the back a tall, impossibly handsome young man with spectacular blue eyes.

Isabella's heart thumped sharply. She felt as if she'd stepped off a clifftop into thin air.

There was no mistaking that face. Every feature was etched on her heart.

'Good heavens, it's Jack!'

Elizabeth's eyes widened. 'Do you know our son?' Her voice was strangely tight.

'Your *son*?'

'Yes,' Elizabeth said, rising to stand beside her. 'That's John Junior. We've always called him Jack.'

Fighting shock, Isabella darted her gaze to the window and its view of the river. What should she say? It was too late to pretend that she didn't know Jack, but why on earth hadn't he told her he was the Kingsley-Lairds' son? 'I—I met him at Pelican's End. Jack was the man who helped me to canoe here.'

'Our Jack was *here*?' Elizabeth cried. To Isabella's dismayed surprise, she dashed to the door and peered down to the river. 'Is he still here?'

'I shouldn't think so. He said he would only wait for half an hour to make sure I was all right.'

Elizabeth looked as if she might cry. 'Why didn't you tell me? Half an hour! If I'd known I could have spoken to him. Oh, dear!' She compressed her lips, but a sob escaped.

'I'm so sorry, Elizabeth. I had no idea Jack was your son. He wouldn't tell me his last name.'

He said he wasn't welcome here.

Her hostess sank onto the nearest chair and covered her face with shaking hands. Isabella felt wretched. Taking a seat beside her, she said quietly, 'I probably owe Jack my life. I hate to think what would have happened if I hadn't found him.'

Elizabeth lowered her hands. Her eyes, as blue as Jack's, were now rimmed with red, and they looked unbearably empty and sad. 'How is my boy?'

'He's very fit and well,' Isabella assured her. And then, wanting to take some of the pain from Jack's mother's eyes, she added, 'He was very good to me.' Oh, heavens, given what had happened this morning, that sounded so coy. 'I—I mean he's a *good* man, Elizabeth.'

Speaking about Jack to his mother caused a sad ache to twist like a thorny vine around her heart.

'I suppose you must think we're a strange family,' Elizabeth said. 'And you'd be right. We have one son and we think the world of him. But we haven't spoken to him for five years.'

'What happened?' Too late, Isabella realised how nosy her question sounded. But she'd been so relieved that Elizabeth seemed unaware of her feelings for her son that she'd asked it without stopping to think.

But, unlike Jack, Elizabeth seemed quite willing to talk about their family's problems. 'Jack and his father had a terrible falling out,' she said. 'My husband has some very set, dare I say *antiquated* ideas about the role of wives, and he made some very cutting, thoughtless comments about Geraldine.'

'Is that Geri? Jack's wife?'

'Yes. John found her too unconventional. He wanted a corporate wife for Jack, someone who'd be happy to support him in his career.

Someone like me, I suppose. You know—a girl who'd hostess important social occasions but stay in the background most of the time. Unfortunately he let Jack know how he felt— that he considered their marriage to be a poor match.' Elizabeth shot Isabella a sharp glance. 'Did Jack tell you about Geri?'

'He only told me that she died.'

'Yes, poor girl. And I'm afraid her death has made any chance of reconciliation less likely.' She released a long, shuddering sigh.

'I take it Jack resented his father's criticism?'

'Oh, absolutely. And I suspect Jack married Geri in response to his father's opposition rather than in spite of it. All the objections his father raised merely strengthened his determination to marry her.' After a pause she added, 'They're both such alpha males neither of them would back down. Jack refused to have anything to do with us while he was married, and then after Geri died he was so angry and hurt it was worse.'

Drawing a lace-edged handkerchief from her skirt pocket, Elizabeth dabbed at her eyes. 'In the end Jack set up his own pastoral company, and for the past two and a half years he's been working in competition with his father.' She almost smiled. 'And doing very well, I might add.'

'I'm sure he misses you.'

Elizabeth looked wistful. 'I'm not surprised he came back to Pelican's End. It's always been a favourite spot, ever since he was a little boy.' Her eyes brightened and she sat straighter. 'I'll wait another day or two, until that creek goes down, and then I might drive up there to visit him.'

Around mid-morning the next day Jack heard the rattle of a low-flying helicopter tracking straight up the course of the river.

He stopped paddling and watched the chopper's approach through squinted eyes. The Killymoon brand was emblazoned on its side and it was dropping lower, as if the pilot planned to land on the bare patch of ground on the adjacent bank.

Jack's stomach took a dive. Almost certainly this meant trouble.

The chopper swooped closer and he recognised the man at the controls. His father. Hell! Definite trouble. Only something damn serious would bring John Kingsley-Laird looking for his son. Could the trouble involve Isabella?

At any other time Jack would have wrestled a man-eating crocodile rather than face up to a reunion with the old man, but today he paddled madly for the shore and clambered up the bank, reaching the chopper as the rotorblades stopped turning. The door of the cockpit opened.

'What are you doing here?' he yelled.

His father didn't answer. Stepping down from the chopper with surprising ease for a man in his late sixties, he stood for a moment, holding his big body braced as if for battle, while his tanned, lined face remained expressionless. 'Good morning, Jack.'

Jack ignored the greeting. 'What are you doing here?' he shouted again. 'What's happened? How's Isabella?'

John Kingsley-Laird shrugged slowly. 'I heard you were on the property. Thought it was about time we spoke a civil word to each other.'

For half a second Jack almost believed him, but then he saw the wary flicker in his father's eyes, quick as a scorpion's tail. Civil? Yeah, right.

'Good morning, Father,' he said with exaggerated politeness. He waited a beat and then added, 'Now, tell me what's happened. Is Isabella OK?'

John's jaw hardened as he shoved his hands into his pockets and rocked back on his heels. 'I imagine she's fine.'

'You *imagine*?' Jack cried. 'What the hell's that supposed to mean?'

'I'm expecting to hear good news—'

'Cut the bull, Father. What the hell are you talking about?'

The older man shifted uncomfortably and crossed his arms over his chest as if to defend himself. 'Isabella was absolutely fine and perfectly happy last night. But when your mother and I woke this morning she wasn't in her room—or anywhere else around the homestead.'

'She's *gone*? Are you saying you've lost her?'

John cleared his throat. 'We heard a helicopter fly overhead earlier, before dawn, but we didn't take any notice. Thought it was probably a contract mustering team heading for White Gums station. But now—ah—we're wondering if perhaps it was people from Amoria.'

Jack groaned and slammed his fist into the palm of his other hand. 'I warned Isabella to be careful. I thought she understood not to speak to *anyone* back at the palace—not until after the wedding day. But she must have told someone. How else could they know where she was?'

John's face took on a greenish cast.

Jack lunged aggressively towards his father. 'What is it? There's something you haven't told me.'

'I—I tried to telephone the King last night.'

'You *what*?' Jack spun away, his hands clenched. God help him, he'd throttle the old guy if he wasn't careful. Just in time he bit back on an urge to curse or lash out. Losing his head wouldn't help anything.

'For God's sake, Jack, I had to try to speak to him. Your mother and I have been invited to the wedding. We were booked to fly out of Darwin today. I couldn't harbour King Albert's daughter under my roof and say nothing!'

'What did he have to say?' Jack asked quietly.

'That's the problem. I couldn't get through to him. But as soon as I mentioned I was ringing about Isabella there was a flurry at the other end, and I was put through to some security fellow. He started to quiz me, but I took exception to his questions and hung up.'

'Didn't Isabella explain to you that her fiancé could have had the line tapped? Damn it, he'd probably already tracked her to Australia. All he needed was a precise location. And you gave it to him on a plate.'

John glared at him. 'Well, that may be so, but what's done is done.'

'I've been such a fool. I should have taken her fears more seriously.' Jack flashed a bitter glance towards his father. 'And I should have realised you'd want to do the macho thing and take over.'

Without meeting his son's gaze, John said grimly, 'I've come here because I guessed you'd want to help her, son.'

Son. That one word falling from his father's lips brought Jack up smartly, as if he'd been lassoed. Until now he'd been trying not to think about the huge effort it must have taken for his father to come after him.

Head down, hands in pockets, he kicked at a dried tuft of grass. 'Thanks—Dad.' He shot a sharp glance his father's way and realised with a shock that the old man was struggling to hide emotions as strong as his own.

'I thought you might want to hightail it over there,' John said grimly. 'You've always been a bit—'

'A bit headstrong? Like you?'

A tremor of a smile twitched John's mouth. 'I was going to say you've always had a strong sense of duty. You're quick to take on responsibilities.'

Mouth tight, jaw squared, Jack couldn't resist a challenge. 'What's this? A character reference after all these years?'

'Maybe. Take it as you like. But I know my son and I know you'll do the right thing, even if it means chasing this girl across the world.'

Jack let out his breath slowly. 'Yes, I'll have to go.'

'But you will be careful, won't you, Jack? Watch your step. You don't know what's behind all this.' John drew a white embossed envelope out of his pocket. 'This is the wedding invitation. It might come in handy—especially as we share the same name.'

'Yeah… Thanks.' Jack took the envelope in his left hand and extended his right hand to shake his father's.

Over their gripped hands their eyes met, and Jack sensed the possibility that five years of animosity might crumble, given the force of the fierce emotion he felt for this old curmudgeon—the same emotion he saw mirrored in his father's eyes.

John blinked. 'You *will* be careful, won't you, son?'

'Don't worry. I'll be careful,' he said.

'It looks like you're dealing with dangerous people.'

Jack frowned. 'Is there something else you haven't told me?'

'I'm afraid we—er—your mother found a hypodermic syringe on the ground outside Isabella's bedroom.'

CHAPTER NINE

'GOOD morning, Your Highness. It's wonderful to see you looking so much better this morning.'

Isabella blinked as a maid swished open her curtains and morning sunlight flooded into her bedroom.

She blinked again…and looked around the room in bewilderment. Tendrils of fear snaked through her.

Nothing was the same as it had been when she went to bed last night. *How odd.* Everything was exactly as it was in her bedroom at home.

The alarm clock she'd had since her thirteenth birthday was sitting on the marble-topped bedside table. The bright silk cushions she'd collected from all over Europe were arranged along the window seat… The oriental carpet on the floor, the smoky-blue velvet curtains and the Tiffany lamp on the antique prayer table in the corner...

She looked down at the long-sleeved silk nightgown she was wearing... *Her* nightgown. How was this possible?

How can these things be in Australia? And why is the maid speaking French?

'How did all these things get here?' she asked, pushing the bedclothes aside. 'These are all *my* things. What are they doing here?' She tried to sit up and was hit by a wave of nauseating dizziness that sent her sinking back to her pillow.

'What a strange question,' the maid said, shaking her head and staring at Isabella with a puzzled smile. 'Why wouldn't your things be here? This is your bedroom.'

'But I'm not in Amoria.' She shot a nervous glance towards the window and her heart lurched when she saw a pale European sky and—oh, help—snowflakes drifting against the angular lines of the Valdenza watchtower.

'Of course you're in Amoria, Your Highness.'

Isabella looked at the maid more carefully—at her icy grey eyes and sharp features—and she was quite sure she'd never seen the woman before. 'Who are you?'

'I'm your nurse.'

'My nurse? But I haven't been ill,' she cried. 'I'm as fit as a fiddle. I've been paddling a canoe. I've been—I'm in Australia—I—I don't understand.'

'Australia? Oh, dear, no. You've been ill in bed for days. Don't you remember anything? You've had a dreadful virus. We've all been out of our minds with worry.' The woman came beside the bed. 'Don't try to talk too much.'

'Where's my own maid, Toinette?'

'Toinette's been assigned to other duties.'

Isabella stared at the woman in horror. Toinette had looked after her all her life.

The nurse laid a cool hand on Isabella's brow. 'At least you don't have a fever any more,' she said. 'But you must rest today. You have to get all your strength back so you'll be strong enough for your wedding tomorrow.'

'*Tomorrow?*' Oh, God. Her heart vaulted. Beneath the sheets her legs began to tremble.

'The whole country has been praying for your recovery,' the nurse added with a smile.

'But I'm not getting married any more. I can't. I mustn't.' Isabella ignored the dizziness and forced herself into a sitting position. 'I want to speak to my father.'

'The King is busy at a very important meeting.'

'This early? Get my brother, then. Let me talk to Danior.' She shot an uneasy glance to her bedside table. 'Where's my telephone? What have you done with it?'

A foxy caution flashed in the nurse's eyes. 'The Count of Montez suggested it would be best if it was removed while you were so ill. He didn't want its ringing to disturb you.'

'Did the Count hire you?' Isabella asked weakly.

'Of course. He's spared no expense. He's a wonderful, wonderful man. You're so lucky. His one desire is to see you well again.'

'I'm well now. I want my telephone back. I demand it. And I want Toinette.'

The woman's right eyebrow lifted. 'I'll have to consult the Count.'

Slumping back against the pillow, Isabella watched the nurse slip out of the room. But the minute she was gone she swung her legs over the side of the bed and, fighting panic and dizziness, forced herself upright.

Oh, Lord, she felt terrible. Dizzy and weak and swamped by fear. She certainly felt as if she'd been ill. Was it possible? Could everything that had happened in Australia been no more than a weird dream? Was Jack a hallucination?

The idea was unbearable.

She stood up gingerly, using the carved cedar post at the end of her bed for support, and once she was steady, she cautiously set out across the room towards the window. The view from the palace offered a stunning vista, clear across the rooftops of Valdenza to the tiered pine forests at the foothills of the Alps and then the towering mountain peaks.

But it wasn't what she wanted to see. Why wasn't she at Killymoon, looking out to the wide brown Pinnaroo River? She was supposed to be dodging the hot Australian sun by sheltering under a wide-brimmed hat. With Jack.

Oh, dear God, surely he wasn't a dream?

She dropped her anxious gaze to the palace courtyard below. There were people everywhere, scurrying through the snow like busy ants. Liveried footmen, warmly clad household servants, uniformed guards—a host of palace employees dashing in and out of the cloisters, the kitchens or the main entrance hall. And no doubt they all had one thing on their minds. The Royal Wedding.

Tomorrow? How could it be tomorrow? Where had the last two days gone?

A wave of nausea rose to her throat. Her legs trembled and she had to grab at the windowsill for support.

This couldn't be happening. She couldn't marry Radik. She mustn't. She wouldn't.

She turned to the long oval mirror in the corner of her room and shuddered at the sight of her reflection. What was the matter with her? Surely she didn't normally look this pale and fragile? And she'd never had those dark circles under her eyes before.

Was she ill?

Her hair was neatly braided into a French plait. Who had done that?

She felt so confused.

Behind her, the door swung open and the Count of Montez strode into her room with his arms outstretched. 'Darling!'

She shuddered.

Dressed in a dark Italian suit, with his black hair smoothly brushed back and an adoring smile pinned in place, Radik looked the perfect royal fiancé.

'It's so good to see you up and about,' he said warmly, taking her hand.

Isabella felt the room sway and he slipped a solicitous arm around her shoulders. 'Take it easy, sweetheart. Here, let me help you back to bed.'

'I'm not ill.' She tried to shout, but her voice was as weak and shaky as her legs.

'That's so good to hear, darling heart.' He pressed dry lips to her brow and she automatically cringed away from his touch. 'Poor lamb, you've had a bad time. It's pre-wedding tension. There have been far too many official engagements.'

He patted her hand. 'But you've been a good girl, and now you're much improved. Nevertheless, you need to take the next twenty-four hours in easy stages.'

He steered her back across the room. Then, with unexpected gentleness, he slipped a hand beneath her knees and lifted her onto the bed. Sitting on the edge of the mattress, he assumed an expression of concerned interest.

'I want to speak to my father,' she said, pushing his hand away when he tried to stroke her.

Ignoring her attempts to brush him off, Radik picked up her hand. 'Of course. I've already sent someone to tell the King the good news of your recovery.'

Isabella looked with distaste as his slim pale fingers enfolded hers. Then she looked more closely at their clasped hands and frowned. Her heart gave a strange little jump when she saw the fingernails of her left hand. Two nails were broken and jagged.

I broke my nails on that first day on the river, when I helped Jack to carry the canoe.

Slipping her right hand under the sheet, she made a surreptitious exploration of her leg. Yes! There were scratch marks on her shins. She'd scratched her legs on lantana bushes when she'd been searching for firewood.

I *have* been in Australia.

The quick leap of excitement faded as she realised this meant she faced a new dilemma. How on earth had Radik transported her back to Amoria without her knowing anything about it?

Oh, dear heaven.

Had she been abducted from Killymoon and then flown back to Amoria? But why couldn't she remember? Had she been drugged?

Her heart thrashed against the wall of her chest like a frightened caged bird. That must be it. She'd been given something to make her forget. That was why she felt so disoriented.

The thought horrified her. 'Radik, please send for a doctor. I must see one. I insist.'

'Calm down, Isabella. You've been receiving the very best medical treatment.'

Was her fiancé holding her prisoner in her own room?

The urge to whip her hand away from his touch was strong. She wanted to leap away from him, to tell him she wouldn't marry him if he was the last man on earth. But then she remembered poor Christos Tenni and the fate he'd met beneath the wheels of a car. Perhaps it was wise to hide that she was frightened and to play along with Radik. She let her hand lie limply inside his.

'I must say I *am* disappointed that my father hasn't come to see me yet,' she said more mildly.

'He was here yesterday.'

'But I don't remember. Why doesn't he come now, if he's been told I'm awake?'

'The King is extremely busy.'

She sighed. 'He always is.' But she suspected Radik had found a way to hold her father at bay.

'He's tied up with important discussions with the EU, but I'm keeping him well informed,' Radik said. 'He understands that you need plenty of rest and he sends you his love.'

'How—how thoughtful.'

'He's proud of you, my dear, and he's especially proud to be attending his only daughter's marriage tomorrow.'

With a supreme effort she fought back another urge to protest. It was hard to think straight, but she was quickly understanding that she needed to stay as calm and clear-headed as possible.

If she made a fuss Radik might sedate her again. That mustn't happen. It was important to stay lucid. And docile. She mustn't arouse his suspicions.

No doubt he planned to keep her here until the wedding ceremony.

He leaned closer and studied her with narrow-eyed wariness. 'Your nurse mentioned that you've been having very strange dreams. She said you thought you'd been to Australia.'

A hectic pulse beat in her throat as his dark eyes pinned her with a piercing cold light. Her chest grew so tight she could hardly breathe.

'Australia?' She frowned. 'I—I was thinking about Australia when I first woke up this morning. But the nurse explained that I'd been ill and—and I realise now that she's right, of course. I know very well that I've never been there.'

Tension seemed to strain from every pore of his skin, drawing his mouth into a thin, downward curving crescent. 'Are you quite clear in your mind about that, Isabella?'

Now her heart hammered a wild tattoo. It thundered in her ears. How should she answer? Was he hoping that she'd forgotten about Australia? Or did he know that was impossible?

She clutched at the bedclothes for support. 'I—I'm so confused, Radik. This past week is a terrible blur. I'm not sure now if I've dreamt things or if they really happened. Can you tell me exactly what I've been doing? I couldn't have been all the way to Australia and back, could I?'

Radik took ages to answer her question. 'You've been behaving very strangely, but everything will be all right very soon,' he said finally.

His eyes glittered from beneath hooded eyes and his forefinger traced a line from her shoulder up her neck to her ear. The rasp of his fingernail felt as threatening as a knife blade. 'Don't be afraid, my sweet. You've no idea how much I'm looking forward to tomorrow.'

No! It can't happen. I can't marry you! I won't. I won't. I won't.

Her mind swam with fear. How on earth could she call off the wedding now? Why, oh, why hadn't she found a way to contact her father last week, when Christos had first warned her of this danger?

She struggled to force her thoughts into order. What could she do? She didn't know what lies her fiancé was feeding her father and brother, but one thing was clear: he planned to prevent her from gaining access to anyone who could call off the wedding. Which meant she was left with only one terrifying alternative.

I will have to let the wedding take place.

Her hand flew to her mouth to hold back a cry of fear. She would have to wait till tomorrow, till she was inside the cathedral. Only then, when she was standing beside her father and surrounded by the bishops and all the European dignitaries, would she be safe from the Count of Montez. He wouldn't be able to do a thing to hurt her.

She would have to speak up then. Oh, Lord. How would she find the strength to call a halt to a royal wedding? Would the people of Amoria ever forgive her? Would her father?

The very thought of having a showdown in public appalled her. It was utterly preposterous. But what was the alternative?

CHAPTER TEN

FOR THE first time since he'd landed in Amoria, Jack was in luck.

He'd half expected to arrive at the cathedral where Isabella was to be married to find that the Cad of Montez had alerted police and the cathedral staff to send him packing. But when he flashed his parents' invitation beneath an usher's nose he was granted immediate access.

Now he was surprised by how calm and quietly confident he felt as he joined the blue-bloods of Europe who were filing up the red carpet and through the huge cathedral doorway.

But there were too many interested glances from the surrounding women. Their heads swivelled so quickly they almost lost their tiaras. It was damn annoying. He was wearing the right clothes—white tie and tails—the same as the rest of the men. Obviously the gene pool for European royalty was so shallow that any new male caused a sensation.

Ignoring their frank, smiling appraisal, and the snooty scowls of the fellows who accompanied them, he followed the usher. His seat was in the middle of a pew, positioned well to the back of the central nave, but it offered a good view of the flower-strewn chancel steps where the ceremony would take place.

As he sat down he looked at the spot where Isabella would stand. And that was when the nerves kicked in.

Beneath his starched collar a film of sweat gathered. His heart raced and his stomach bunched into knots.

He looked around him and his throat tightened as he studied the gothic splendour of the cathedral's magnificent interior. Soaring vaulted ceilings, huge stained glass windows above the altar, an enormous pipe organ.

He couldn't imagine a more imposing and dignified scene. Not a great setting for creating a scandal.

He prayed for some kind of divine inspiration.

Or, better still, divine intervention.

Only a miracle could save Isabella now. A miracle…or *Jack*… But how could he, a mere commoner from Down Under, stop her wedding?

The worst of it was he had no idea of Isabella's condition. How was she feeling? What did she remember? If he could only take hold of her, look into her eyes.

There was so little he could do.

And he was so afraid for her.

When the police in Darwin had tested the syringe his parents had found, they'd reported that it contained traces of hypnotic drugs, including scopolamine—a drug thieves used to rob unsuspecting tourists.

But the Amorian police hadn't believed Jack's claim that their princess had been abducted from Australia.

'That's impossible! Her Royal Highness hasn't been out of the country,' they'd insisted.

'In fact she's been ill and confined to the palace since last Friday.'

He had created a scene. Which hadn't helped matters. The police had decided he was a crazy ratbag from Down Under and had thrown him out with a warning. And there'd been no chance of support from the palace. Isabella's fiancé seemed to have total control of the situation, and all Jack's efforts to make any kind of contact with the King or Prince Danior had been blocked.

Now he scanned the members of the congregation in the pews around him and tried to identify the people trained to intercept anyone approaching the Princess. Security would still be tight. There were sure to be operatives discreetly positioned amongst the wedding guests.

Normally a church could be relied on as a sanctuary, where weapons were not allowed, but there were so many Heads of State and VIPs present that Jack suspected that with one wrong move he could be shot.

Isabella was ready.

The princess bride—dressed in a breathtak-

ingly beautiful gown of silver French brocade.
Her dark hair was threaded with orange blossoms and she wore a medieval veil held in
place by her mother's diamond tiara.

Diamonds sparkled at her ears, around her
neck and on her breast. In her arms she carried
a bouquet of white lilies of the valley, floral
symbols of virtue and fertility.

Every detail of her appearance spelled royal
romance.

And, although she hadn't yet seen them, she
knew that in the adjacent rooms her six bridesmaids were ready and waiting, dressed in
white gowns of silk organza and carrying arm-
fuls of snowy white roses.

In the palace ballrooms in the West Wing,
the Master of the Household would be deliv-
ering a final briefing to the under-butler, the
wine-butler, the pages and the footmen, to ensure that the wedding breakfast would be
served with the precision of a military ma-
noeuvre.

In front of the palace steps open carriages were lined up, waiting to take her and her attendants through the streets of Valdenza past cheering citizens. To the cathedral.

And all Isabella could think of was Jack.

She longed for him. Longed for him with an ache that brought a sharp pain to her chest and tears to her eyes.

All night she'd tossed and turned, reliving every moment of their adventure on the river...remembering again the sexy warmth of his mouth...the heated mystery of his touch...the wonder of his hands gliding over her skin...the soul-shattering passion of their bodies joining in intimate communion.

She *loved* him.

Not merely because he'd rescued her and protected her. And made love to her. She loved the man. And she loved the person she became when she was with him.

Now, as she stood at the window in her wedding gown, taking one last look at her beloved city, the lilies in her arms trembled.

* * *

Jack heard the sound of deafening cheers outside the cathedral. It meant that Isabella had arrived. His heart pounded. Hot and cold chills chased up and down his spine. The cheering of the crowds swelled to a roar. His stomach clenched tighter and he reached into his trouser pocket for a handkerchief to mop his brow.

All too soon, another fanfare of trumpets announced the bride's arrival at the cathedral door. The congregation rose. A sea of heads turned towards the main entrance.

Organ music filled the cathedral and Jack's breath seemed to drain from his body as he turned and saw Isabella framed in the cathedral doorway. She looked so beautiful his mouth turned dry as dust. But she looked different— palely luminous, ethereal, other-worldly—as if she was walking in a dream.

His heart thumped like a locomotive piston. How had his week of solitude in the hut at Pelican's End brought him to *this*?

Isabella wished for numbness. She didn't want to feel anything. Not this awful fear. Not this ghastly sickness in her stomach. The trembling trepidation in her limbs, the dryness in her mouth and the shocking, panicky interruptions to her breathing.

Her attendants were making her even more anxious as they whispered and fussed nervously with her dress and train. She forced herself to drag in a long, deep breath and to let it out slowly. The deep breath helped a little, and she repeated the process.

Perhaps that was what she should do to keep her terror at bay. She should focus on her breathing. On that and nothing else.

That way she could close herself off from the hundreds of watching eyes. She would take two steps while she breathed in…another two as she breathed out.

Slow breathing and steady steps…they would propel her down the aisle.

'It's time to go, Your Highness.'

Oh, help! This was it. The moment she'd been dreading. Her father was waiting for her halfway down the aisle. In accordance with Amorian tradition, she had to make the first part of the journey by herself. She drew in a breath and forced a shaky foot forward. *Don't look to the left or right. Breathe in...* She stepped inside the cathedral. *Breathe out...*

It was happening. She was moving down the aisle towards her father. *Mustn't think. Just breathe. Don't think.*

Around and above her the loud organ music swelled to a crescendo. *Breathe, and then take a step.* The procession continued, and in what seemed like no time at all there were only two more steps till she reached her father. It seemed like years since she'd seen him. He held out a hand to her.

'Hello, my dear.' His voice was rich and low, softened by emotion.

Was he smiling? She couldn't tell. Her vision was blurred by the sudden rush of tears to her eyes.

Her father stepped closer, took her arm and slipped it through his, ready to progress with her to the very front of the cathedral. To Radik.

Isabella stood still.

'Let's go,' the King murmured.

Her heart seemed to stop, but then it picked up pace and began to thunder in her ears. 'No,' she whispered.

She felt rather than saw her father's frown. Then the pressure of his hand around her arm tightened and he tried to guide her forward. 'Come on, Isabella.'

'No.' Oh, God. Was she strong enough to stand up to this man? He'd dominated and ruled her life. 'I'm not going any further,' she said. 'I can't marry Radik.'

She felt the sudden tension in him. A terrible stillness. Felt fear as the grip on her arm turn to steel. 'Isabella, pull yourself together.' The King forced the command through gritted teeth.

'Father, please don't make me go any further.'

'What's come over you? This is nonsense.'

In spite of the loud organ music she heard a rustling of confused whispers spreading through the rows of people on either side of the aisle.

She looked down the nave and saw Radik at the front of the church. He was frowning, staring back at them with an intent, hard look.

'Are you still feeling ill?' the King asked, a little more kindly, almost hopefully. 'Lean on me.'

'I'm not ill, Father. I'm sorry to do this to you, but I have no choice. I refuse to be married today.'

Another frantic glance towards Radik showed her that his face had grown red. He looked as if he was about to charge down the aisle towards her. Did she have to shout her refusal? Could Radik and her father force this wedding?

There was a momentary pause in the music and she heard a different sound, a swelling of surprised, excited murmurs. And footsteps. Men's raised voices. A scuffle?

Then came the sound of another voice. A familiar voice calling, *'Carmen!'*

A tremor shook Isabella from head to toe. 'Jack?'

Was she dreaming? How could Jack be here? The last time she'd seen him he'd been about to paddle back to Pelican's End.

Swinging out of her father's grasp, she turned. *And saw him.* He was making his way down the aisle towards her, dragging two security guards as if they were nothing more than angry, snarling terrier pups attached to his clothing.

Jack. His blazing blue eyes were fixed on her. He looked fiercely determined. He looked wonderful. Surrounded by a scattering bevy of shocked, pale bridesmaids, he looked fabulously suntanned. Gloriously out of place.

Isabella was shaking—stunned—happy and scared at once.

'This is outrageous,' the King cried. 'Guards, arrest that man!'

'No!' shouted Isabella.

The aisle was filling with men in uniform.

'No!' she shouted again.

The organ music stopped abruptly on a discordant note. Heart racing, Isabella lifted her heavy skirt and began to hurry back down the aisle towards Jack. She was aware of a shocked collective gasp from the congregation. And the King hurrying after her.

Throwing a frantic glance back over her shoulder, she saw Radik storming after her father. And, behind him, a startled bishop.

The urge to hurl herself into Jack's arms was overwhelming. She wanted to fall against his shoulder and cling to him, to feel the lovely solid strength that she'd always found in his arms.

But he was in the fierce grip of security men and it was impossible. Their eyes met, and Isabella felt an exquisite thrill tremble through her.

'Who are you?' King Albert demanded, glowering at Jack.

Despite the strong hold of his captors, Jack squared his shoulders. He met the monarch's enraged glare with a level, cool gaze. 'Your Majesty, I'm Jack Kingsley-Laird,' he said, speaking in English.

'John and Elizabeth's son? From Australia?'

Her father's eyes narrowed as he darted a swift glance towards Isabella and then focused once more on Jack. 'And what is the meaning of this unforgivable disruption?'

'Your daughter needs my help, sir. And yours.'

'What absolute nonsense.'

'Please ask her,' Jack insisted.

'It's true, Father,' cried Isabella. 'I must talk to you. I can't—'

'Don't listen to them.' Radik elbowed his way into the middle of the gathering. Beneath his slick black hair his face was as white and cold as a snow-covered mountain, and his entire frame quivered with anger as he pointed an accusing finger towards Jack. 'I demand that this criminal be thrown out of here and that the ceremony continues immediately.'

Isabella felt dizzy as she looked around at the circle of faces—at Jack's bristling determination, at her father's dismayed disbelief and the bishop's shock. At Radik's fury.

'It's too late, Radik,' she said quietly, but her heart was beating so wildly she feared she might faint. 'I'm not going to marry you.'

Horrified gasps seemed to echo in waves through the cathedral.

To the King, she said, 'Please, Father, you have to stop this wedding. I can't go ahead with it.'

'But, Isabella—'

'Please,' she insisted, more forcefully. She didn't dare look at Radik again.

'Are you sure?' the King whispered.

'I'm sorry, Father, but, yes, I'm very, very sure. I can explain.'

For an interminable stretch of time no one moved or spoke. But then the King nodded slowly. 'Very well,' he said, his gaze resting briefly on Isabella, then for a longer time on Jack. Finally he looked towards Radik. He frowned and shook his head. 'We had better discuss this in the vestry.'

To the bishop, he said, 'I'm sorry, your Grace, but you'll have to announce a short adjournment of these proceedings.'

By the time Isabella and Jack had told their story to King Albert he looked like an old and defeated man—lost and bewildered.

'How could Radik have deceived me?' he murmured, shaking his head sadly. 'I had such high hopes for him. He had such interesting schemes for our estates.'

The King sat staring into space for several long minutes, but at last he snapped out of his gloom and became businesslike again. 'I can see I have no choice,' he said. 'The ceremony must be cancelled. The bishop will have to handle that.'

Isabella closed her eyes as relief washed through her.

Her father rose stiffly to his feet. 'This has been a direct attack on the royal household. Radik must be brought in. I need to talk to my chief of police about poor Dr Tenni's death.' He crossed to the vestry door. 'And I'll need the palace secretary to handle the fall-out from this crisis.' He sighed deeply. 'What a mess. The guests will go into turmoil.'

'I'm sorry, Father. If I had been able to contact you straight away we could have called this off a week ago.'

His eyes regarded her sadly, but he didn't give her the absolution she longed for.

How silly of her to think that this morning's revelations might have softened her father's attitude. He hadn't changed. There was every chance he would never realise that this morning's fiasco mightn't have happened if he'd been more willing to talk to her—if he hadn't been such a difficult man to approach, even at the best of times.

He went to the door to speak to the guard posted outside and Isabella turned quickly to Jack. Throughout this session she had been greedily stealing chances to look at him—admiring the distinctive jut of his nose, the familiar, unsettling gleam in his blue eyes, the darkness of his skin, tanned by his life in the Outback, the grave, straight line of his mouth.

Having him here now made up for every horror she'd suffered. She longed to be alone with him, to feel his reassuring touch, to thank him for coming so bravely to her rescue. But he remained remote, sitting some distance away from her and paying her no more than polite attention. She felt the gap between them keenly.

'Isabella,' came her father's voice, snapping her out of her reverie. 'I think it's time you went back to the palace now. There are matters I need to discuss with Mr Kingsley-Laird.'

Matters to discuss? What matters? I need to talk to Jack, too. She was being dismissed like a child.

'Run along, my dear,' the King said.

Her nervous fingers pleated the stiff silver brocade of her skirt and she looked hopefully towards Jack. But he was watching her father with a disturbingly grave expression.

'Does this discussion involve me?' she asked, forcing her chin defiantly high.

The King's jaw dropped as if he couldn't believe that his normally submissive daughter had questioned him. 'It does,' he said.

Until that moment she had thought that the worst was over. She had been feeling almost normal again. But now she felt a fresh stab of dismay.

'Then I'd like to stay.'

On the other side of the room Jack made an uncomfortable throat-clearing sound, and when she darted another look his way he frowned at her and shook his head. He was dismissing her too!

This was too much! Why did she have to live her life surrounded by men with god-complexes? She wanted to stamp her foot, to throw a tantrum. 'Surely I'm entitled to know what you're going to discuss about me?'

The King sighed loudly. 'How can you be so obtuse, Isabella? From what I've heard of your time in Australia, and from what I've seen with my own eyes this morning, it's clear that I need to ask Mr Kingsley-Laird about his intentions.'

She gasped.

Jack flinched as if he'd been slapped in the face. The muscles in his throat worked. 'My intentions?' he repeated faintly.

'Exactly,' replied the King. 'You've come from the other side of the world to hijack my daughter's wedding. I understand that your prime motive was Isabella's safety, but I can't believe you would have gone to such lengths if you didn't have strong feelings for her.'

A wave of embarrassing heat flooded Isabella and she closed her eyes. How could her father do this? He was putting Jack through hoops like a suitor caught in a compromising situation. She felt wretched—as if she'd unwittingly led her valiant rescuer into a trap.

The King hurried on. 'My daughter spent several days alone in your company. I'm sure there are things about this relationship that I should know.'

'Father!' she cried, so horrified and embarrassed she wanted to slide under the carpet. 'I think you're jumping to conclusions.'

'Am I?' the King demanded. His eyebrows rose as he shifted a shrewd glance from one to the other. 'Am I?' he repeated.

Jack cleared his throat. 'Your Majesty, Isabella and I haven't discussed—er—I mean—regarding my intentions, I haven't—' He broke off.

Isabella covered her face with her hands. She couldn't bear this. Jack had rushed over

to this country to save her. But that didn't con-
stitute *intentions*. Not the kind her father was
suggesting. Not a marriage proposal.

Heaven knew, she'd been thrilled beyond
belief to see him in the cathedral. Her first
thought had been that he loved her as fiercely
as she loved him, that he'd come all this way
to do more than rescue her. To declare his feelings.

But now the granite-hard look on Jack's
face told her that she'd been overly romantic
to imagine he loved her. He hadn't changed
his mind since they'd parted at Killymoon.

She couldn't bear to listen while he told her
father about his *lack* of intentions. It would be
easier for everyone if she wasn't present.

'Perhaps I *should* leave,' she said in a small,
tight voice.

The men eyed each other solemnly, then
nodded.

With a choked, angry cry, she rushed out of
the room.

The King's lips pursed thoughtfully as he
watched the door swing shut. His eyes met

Jack's. 'I must ask you to put yourself in my position,' he said. 'I've had a shock this morning. I've learned that I've let down my only daughter rather badly. I didn't see what lay under my very nose. Isabella had to cross oceans to find safety and it took a total stranger to come to her rescue.'

'The circumstances—' Jack began, but the King cut him off with a flourish of his hand.

The royal complexion darkened. 'Since my wife died I haven't been a good father.'

Wisely, Jack didn't comment. He was thinking of the pain in Isabella's eyes when she'd left.

'Radik might have pulled the wool over my eyes, but I had both eyes wide open this morning,' King Albert continued. 'I saw you struggling with those guards in the cathedral, but I didn't sense threat or anger from you. All I saw was concern for Isabella. And desire. And there was the same response from my daughter.'

'Your daughter is a wonderful person, sir.'

'If I achieve nothing else,' her father said, 'I want to ensure her ongoing safety and happiness.'

'Yes.' Jack managed to squeeze the word past the tightness in his throat. 'That's very understandable.' Feeling like a guilty criminal, he dropped his gaze. He wanted to assure Isabella's father that his intentions were honourable, but right at this moment it was hard to get his thoughts past the fact that he'd stolen her virginity. And on that very same day he'd abandoned her.

Did he have the right to offer her ongoing safety and happiness? Was he any more worthy of her than the Cad of Montez?

'I'm an Australian, and a mere commoner,' he reminded the King.

'I'm aware of that, but it's most unlikely that Isabella will ever ascend to the throne. And you come from fine stock.' A flicker of a smile tweaked King Albert's mouth. 'Your family is about as high up the gum tree as Australian society tolerates, isn't it?'

Without waiting for an answer he stepped forward and slapped Jack on the shoulder. 'But perhaps I'm jumping the gun. You said that you and Isabella haven't discussed your plans. Well—go after her and talk to her. I'll give you till this evening.'

'This evening, sir?'

'You can come to the palace for dinner and I'll expect your answer then.' Turning abruptly, King Albert opened the door, and immediately the swarm of people waiting outside clamoured to speak to him. Over his shoulder he said to Jack, 'I dine at eight.'

CHAPTER ELEVEN

ISABELLA lay in a wretched huddle on top of her bedspread, dressed only in her petticoat and surrounded by a sea of sodden, crumpled tissues.

A maid tiptoed into the room. 'Your Highness,' she said softly, 'are you receiving visitors?'

Isabella moaned. 'No-o-o! I've told you, I can't possibly see anyone.'

She wanted to stay in this darkened bedroom for ever, away from prying eyes, wrapped in misery. Surely after everything she'd been through she deserved a good long cry? She was so angry with her father. The man had the sensitivity of a bulldozer. How could he have thrown those blunt questions at Jack? Couldn't he see that he was forcing the poor man into a corner?

And what on earth was he plotting? Why did she have to have a king for a father? Oh, God, already she was losing control of her life again.

The maid hovered uncertainly by the bed. 'Do you want me to deliver a message, Your Highness?'

Isabella groaned impatiently. Where was her *old* maid? Toinette would know what to do without asking these endless, tiresome questions.

'No, there's no message,' she cried, reefing another tissue from the box and blowing her nose loudly. 'Just offer my apology, say I'm indisposed and send any visitors away.'

Perched on the edge of an antique sofa in the Princess's sitting room, Jack eased his stiff collar away from his neck. He'd come straight from the cathedral to the palace without changing out of his formal clothes and his tie was strangling him. Nerves bunched in his stomach, and with a restless sigh he rose and crossed the Wedgwood-blue carpet to the window.

Outside snowflakes drifted down from a pale, chilly sky. He thrust his hands deep into his trouser pockets and flexed his shoulders as he watched the snow spread lacy shawls across the ancient cobbled courtyard. Beyond the palace gates the snow glittered over the winter-grey city, covering Valdenza's landscape with spotless beauty.

It was as pure and white as Isabella had been when she'd entered the cathedral this morning. His throat stung as he remembered how unbelievably beautiful she'd looked.

He'd been terrified as he watched her take those first steps down the aisle. Terrified that she was heading to her doom and that he would be powerless to help. But what had terrified him most was the discovery that Amoria's beloved Princess Isabella had broken through the careful wall he'd built around his heart. *He loved her.*

He'd been working hard to deny it—it was totally inappropriate—but he *loved* her. His lovely, courageous, gypsy princess had brought him back to life—brought him the happiness he'd considered forever lost.

He loved her in spite of his fears—in spite of the horror of losing Geri and his unwillingness to risk the pain of losing his heart to another woman.

No doubt it had happened long ago—long before that fateful morning on the riverbank when they made love. Perhaps he'd fallen for her right back on that very first night in the hut…

All he knew now was that he was deeply, irreversibly in love. And she was safe. And her father had asked a question he hadn't been prepared to ask himself.

What *were* his intentions?

A soft groan broke from his lips and a horrible heaviness grew inside him as he stared at the snow-covered landscape. How could he ask Isabella to leave all this? Her homeland was like a grand old lady—dignified and genteel and steeped in tradition.

He couldn't imagine a scene more different from the hard red Outback of Northern Australia. By comparison the unkempt country where he spent most of his time was as rough and untamed as a badly brought up youth.

What could he offer her besides complications?

If he asked her to marry him he would have to ask her to divide her time between two countries...two worlds...two allegiances...

A sound behind him brought him whirling around, and his heart thudded as he turned to greet her. Would he find the right words to convince her?

To his surprise he saw that it was only the plain little servant who'd come through the doorway. She was looking very glum and shaking her head at him.

Isabella lifted her head from her damp pillow and tried to look grateful as the maid placed a cup and saucer carefully on the bedside table. 'Thank you.' She sniffed.

The girl stood by the bed, her hands plucking at her apron. 'I hope you don't mind, Your Highness, but there's a gentleman caller who won't take no for an answer.'

Isabella's head snapped up. 'Gentleman? What gentleman?'

'He said he was your doctor, and he insisted he *must* see you.'

'My doctor?' Isabella repeated, frowning at the girl. 'I don't understand.'

The maid's eyes grew round. 'I must say I thought it was strange for you to have a foreign doctor, ma'am.'

'A foreign—' An alarmed kind of excitement skittered through her. 'What—what kind of foreigner is he?'

'I'm not sure. He speaks English, but he doesn't sound English, if you know what I mean.'

'Oh, good heavens, it must be Jack!' Isabella leapt to her feet and grabbed the maid by the elbows. 'Are you telling me Jack's here? In the palace?'

The girl looked frightened. 'He called himself Dr Kingsley-Laird.'

'Oh, my God!' Isabella's heart crashed against her chest like a wave breaking on a sandbar. 'Where is he now?'

'I'm afraid he's right outside this door.'

She dashed towards the door, but halfway across the room she caught sight of herself in the mirror. Her nose and her eyes were red and swollen and her cheeks were streaked with mascara. 'Oh, no! I look like a scarecrow after a hailstorm.'

Spinning around, she headed instead for her bathroom. 'Tell him I'll be ready in five minutes.' Her mind was whirring so wildly she couldn't grasp at a single thought before it slipped away again.

Why had Jack come? What had he told her father? Oh, dear, her father hadn't forced him to come to her, had he?

Her hands shook as she cleaned the make-up from her face and tried not to think about the closed, wary look on Jack's face when her father had asked him his intentions.

She splashed her skin with cold water, desperate to flush away the evidence of her tears. With frantic, trembling fingers she tugged the orange blossoms from her hair, then dragged her brush through the tangles with savage thrusts, not caring how much it hurt.

What had Jack come to tell her? It couldn't possibly be good news, could it? She was sure her feelings for him would never be returned.

In her bedroom again, she threw open her wardrobe doors and began to hunt through the racks of expensive garments, searching for the right thing to wear. What would Jack like? Oh, dear heaven.

Behind her, the door opened.

'Your five minutes are up,' said a deeply masculine voice.

Her hands flew to her chest as she whirled around. Jack strode into the room, looking so tall and splendid she wanted to throw herself into his arms. *But she had no idea why he'd come.*

'I—I'm not quite ready,' she stammered, feeling foolish as she stood there with her arms crossed over the lace-trimmed neckline of her silk petticoat.

He flashed her a fleeting, crooked smile. 'A petticoat is an improvement on my old shirt.'

Her attempt to return his smile was even more shaky than his. 'It's very impertinent of you to barge into my bedroom under false pretences, *Doctor*.'

'I had to see you.'

'Your talk with my father—the discussion I wasn't allowed to hear. What did he say? Has he sent you here?'

'Well—sort of—I mean no, Isabella. The King did tell me to come to speak to you, but I—I wanted to come anyway.'

Did you, Jack? His words brought a momentary rush of relief, but her hope faded when she saw how strained and tense he still looked—as formidable and rock-like as the cliffs that stood sentry over the Pinnaroo River. It wasn't the look of a man who had come to her willingly or gladly.

It was how he'd looked when they'd parted at Killymoon.

Despite her scanty clothing, she tried to look dignified as she pointed to the sofa on the far wall. 'Please take a seat. Just push the cushions aside.'

She chose the small chair that stood in the corner and felt as tense and scared as Jack looked.

They stared at each other across the room. Isabella dampened her dry lips with her tongue. 'I haven't thanked you for what you did this morning. You can't imagine how relieved I was to hear you call out to me in the cathedral.'

He smiled again, but he didn't look any more relaxed. 'I had to come. I couldn't have sat there at Pelican's End once I'd learned that you'd been drugged and kidnapped.'

'How did you find out? Did your parents contact you?'

He nodded. 'Perhaps the one good thing that's come out of this is that my father and I are talking again.'

'I'm so pleased.' She took a deep breath. 'Is that the only good thing, Jack?'

'You're safe from Radik. That's the very best thing.'

'Yes.'

She rubbed her arms. Her room was heated but she felt suddenly cold. 'You must forgive my father's bossiness,' she said, anxious to fill any gaps in the conversation. 'He's so used to giving orders on a daily basis that he forgets he shouldn't boss people around in his personal life.'

'The poor man's had a major shock this morning. You can't blame him for quizzing me when I came charging after you from the other side of the world.'

'He didn't expect you to tell him—about—?'

His eyes seemed to pierce her. 'About personal details of our time together?'

She nodded, and hoped that the blush she was feeling didn't show.

'No, Isabella.'

'But he wants to know your intentions?' Her hands twisted nervously on her lap.

'Yes. And he's expecting my answer by dinner this evening.'

'This evening?' She knew she sounded frightened and she looked away from him, concentrating instead on a crushed orange blossom that had fallen to the floor. 'What—what have you told him so far?'

'I couldn't in all conscience discuss such a private matter with anyone else when I haven't discussed it with you.'

'But you have, haven't you?' Sudden tears stung her eyes and she blinked them away. This was awful.

Her heart raced, and although she didn't lift her gaze she sensed his escalating tension. He was sitting very stiffly on the edge of the sofa.

'I haven't—'

'It's OK, Jack,' she cut in, stopping his words with an outstretched hand. 'I understand that you don't have *intentions*. Not the kind my father was hinting at. You came here to help me because you're a good man—a *gallant* man—but I know you have no plans for our future. You explained it all at Killymoon. So

it's OK; you don't have to say it again. I'd
rather you didn't. You can go. I'll tell my father that you came here, as he asked, and that
you spoke to me and—and that everything's
settled.'

Jack was on his feet, crossing the room.
'Isabella, stop babbling and give me a chance
to speak.'

'No!' she cried. 'It's all right. You don't
need to. It was only a matter of days ago when
you stood on the riverbank and told me *exactly*
why we have no future. You said we come
from two different worlds. I understand that,
and if you don't mind—I'd rather not hear it
again.'

'Not if I've changed my mind?'

Her head shot up. 'What?' Jack's blue eyes
were shimmering. He was looking at her with
a strangely twisted, almost sad little smile.

'My dear girl, I came here to ask if you'd
do me the great honour of marrying me.'

Oh, no, Jack, no. Not now. Not like this.

Suddenly ill, she dropped her face into her
hands. *Now she knew why he'd looked so
scared. This was terrible.*

'Isabella?'

It was wrong, so wrong. Her father had ordered Jack to propose. She hadn't even finished changing her clothes after one disastrous interrupted wedding, and already another poor man was being pressured into marrying her.

'I—I thought you cared for me,' he said, standing close beside her chair.

'I do, but—'

His hand reached down and he touched her cheek gently. 'You know I need you.'

Yes…she knew that from the way he'd made love to her. But he'd loved her with the unleashed passion of a man who'd been too long without a woman. That didn't mean…

'Carmen,' he whispered.

'Don't call me that.'

'I know it won't be easy for you to adjust to the kind of marriage I'm offering. We'd have to find a way to merge our two completely different lifestyles. But I think we could do it. I have a very comfortable house in Perth. I can appoint someone to take over many of my current responsibilities, and now that my parents and I are reconciled—'

'Don't, Jack, please.'

'Don't *what*?' he cried as his hands closed around her arms and he hauled her to her feet.

Their faces were inches apart and her heart rocked wildly. *Don't ask me to marry you because you think you must—to do the right thing.*

'Don't make an emotional commitment sound so businesslike and so—so *logical*.'

She heard the impatient rasp of his sigh. He picked up a loose curl of her hair and rolled it between a finger and thumb. Her breathing seemed to stop as he stared at it. 'OK, let's drop the logic,' he murmured, threading his hand more deeply into her curls, taking a big handful of hair and drawing her head back so that her face was tilted to his.

How could she resist Jack? How could she hold back from the seduction of his warm, sexy lips—or the taste of him—that heady, familiar flavour that was purely Jack? Against her will she felt her body stirring—stomach tightening and limbs melting.

But, no. No! She was too easily seduced by this man.

It would be bliss to give in to him. But she mustn't. She'd learned a hard lesson from her narrow escape with Radik. When she'd been engaged to him there'd been no talk of love, and now Jack hadn't mentioned it either.

Her heart felt as if it were breaking as she stiffened in his arms.

'Isabella, what's the matter?'

She longed to tell him. It would be so simple to say *I need you to say that you love me.* But if she had to ask…

Pride held her tongue. Pride and common sense. She might be able to induce Jack to say the words, but it would be as bad as her father persuading him to come to her.

Jack couldn't love her the way she needed him to. He'd told her how very deeply he'd loved Geri. If he felt that way now he would have said so, without having to be asked.

The knowledge was killing her.

'What is it, Isabella?'

'I'm sorry, Jack.'

'Sorry?' She felt him freeze with shock.

'I don't want you to kiss me. I want you to go away.'

'You don't mean that.'

'Yes, I do.'

'Are you sure?'

She opened her mouth to say yes, but the word wouldn't come out. Pressing her lips together, she nodded.

'Say it, Isabella.' His voice was rough, choked. Angry. 'Say the words. Tell me you won't marry me. Tell me to leave.'

The tears she'd been trying so hard to hold back forced their way into her eyes. 'Please,' she whispered.

'Say it.'

'Please…leave.'

'But you're crying. I don't understand.'

Go, Jack, go. Go now, before I break down and make an utter fool of myself.

She drew in a deep, shuddering breath, gathering just enough strength for this last ordeal.

'I'm very grateful for *all* your help. I really am. But I'd like you to leave now.' Feeling ill and icy cold, she forced herself to cross the room to the door. 'I'll give Father your answer,' she said softly as she opened the door. 'I'll explain.'

Please, don't look so shocked.

He looked pale beneath his tan. 'Is this goodbye, Carmen?'

'Yes. Goodbye, Jack.'

Slowly, *too slowly*, he walked towards the door. She heard the tortured rasp of his indrawn breath as he passed her, and the sharp click as he closed the door behind him, and then her tears began to fall.

'More coffee, sir?' The airline flight attendant leaned over Jack, brandishing a coffee pot.

'Thanks,' he muttered, raising his cup to be refilled, although he doubted that an overdose of caffeine would give him the lift he needed.

He felt wretched. He'd totally stuffed everything. Everything about the meeting with Isabella had been a first-class fiasco. What a fool he'd been. Had there ever in the history of man been a more stupid, rushed, pathetic proposal?

He shouldn't have responded with such a knee-jerk reaction to the pressure from her father. He should have taken more time. Expressed his feelings better. Opened up to the woman he loved.

Problem was, he'd become socially incompetent since Geri's death. He'd spent too much time with his thoughts and emotions locked up—isolated himself as effectively as if he'd set up permanent camp in a remote gorge in the wilderness.

And he'd spent so much effort convincing Isabella that a relationship with him was hopeless that he couldn't reasonably expect her to accept a sudden change of attitude. It was impossible for her to understand the courage it had taken to risk his heart and propose to another woman.

But, damn it, getting onto this plane and taking off from Valdenza's airport, knowing that he was leaving her behind, was the hardest thing he'd ever done. The thought of returning to Australia without her, of never seeing her again, was unbearable.

He was drowning in memories, torturing himself by lingering over every disturbing detail of her loveliness—of how she'd looked in that silken petticoat, with her dark hair falling around her shoulders in a shining tumble. He could still see her faultless complexion, the dusky pink of her lips, the flecks of ebony in her beautiful dark eyes...

His body ached for her. His blood leapt with the memory of their time on the river—of her soft, warm lips locked with his, of her pliant, urgent body lifting beneath his.

But the worst memory was seeing her turning away from him...showing him the door...

And here he was, sipping coffee as his plane cruised somewhere over the Russian steppes on its way to Tokyo and then on to northern Australia.

Isabella and Amoria were far behind him. Gone. Out of his life. The tiny glimmer of hope that he might have a second chance at happiness had been snuffed out. And somehow he had to go on living—surviving—just as he had for the past three years.

Jack was back in hell.

CHAPTER TWELVE

'MR KINGSLEY-LAIRD, it's so good to see you.' The matron bustled forward as the sliding glass doors of the Royal Perth Hospital parted to admit Jack.

'I'm sorry I'm running late. My meeting ran over time.'

His excuse was greeted by a coy smile. 'I'm sure you're a very busy man. There's no need to apologise—besides, it's not every day we receive such a magnificent donation for women's and children's health services. Now, if you'll come this way, please, everyone is ready and waiting.'

Jack paid scant attention to his surroundings as the matron escorted him down endless corridors. Even though he'd visited several hospitals in the past few months, he still felt a need to avert his eyes from the sight of medical equipment and bedridden patients.

And he resisted thinking too hard about the reason behind his new interest in giving donations to hospitals, but he suspected that at some subconscious level he was trying to buy back happiness.

After too many lonely pre-dawn hours spent staring out at the lightening sky, he could only hope that doing something good—giving away bucketloads of money—would ease the new pain that had lain like a cold and empty hollow around his heart ever since he'd returned from Amoria.

'We're almost there,' the matron said, as if she sensed his growing tension.

He shook his head clear of the thoughts that shadowed him constantly these days and forced his attention to the bright murals on the walls of the ward they were passing. 'These look terrific,' he said, pointing to a colourful jungle scene.

'Yes,' the matron agreed. 'We have a wonderful new volunteer who's doing amazing things in the children's ward.'

As she spoke she nodded towards her right, and Jack followed the direction of her gaze. He caught a glimpse of a woman's dark hair. He looked again. She was sitting beside a bed on the far side of the ward, waggling a fluffy green puppet at a little girl who had both legs in plaster.

He stopped dead in his tracks. *'Isabella.'* The name burst from him like an arrow from a crossbow.

His companion looked understandably surprised. 'Do you know our delightful Isabella?' she asked.

'It can't be her,' he whispered, moving towards the ward doorway.

The child in the bed was grinning up at the woman.

It *was* Isabella. *His* Isabella. He could see her profile as she smiled at the child. Smiled that lovely, sparkling-eyed, dimpling smile he knew so well.

How could this be? What was she doing here?

He'd kept abreast of events in Amoria. He knew that Radik was in prison. Isabella was supposed to be working in Amorian hospitals, seeking a life of privacy.

A horrible coldness swept through him. Why on earth had she come to Australia without contacting him? *He had to talk to her.*

There was so much he needed to tell her… so much to undo.

He wasn't sure how long he might have stood there staring if the matron hadn't tapped him on the shoulder.

'Mr Kingsley-Laird, we're behind schedule,' she said.

'But I know that woman. I know Isabella. I have to talk to her.'

For the first time the matron's pleasant demeanour faltered. 'I'm afraid everyone's waiting, sir.' Years spent instilling the fear of God into young nurses had lent her voice a chilling edge. 'The Premier is already here—and the chairman of the board—all the press people. We're running *late*.'

'Yes, of course,' Jack muttered, quickly suppressing a sigh. 'Let's get on with the formalities.' *Then I'll find Isabella.*

In the reception room, beaming smiles and goodwill abounded.

Frustratingly long speeches were made, but at last Jack was able to hand a cheque to the hospital board's chairman. Cameras flashed, and there were more flashes as he shook hands with the Premier, board members, the doctors and the matron.

Journalists pushed forward, asking questions…

Jack turned to the nearest doctor. 'I'd like to make a quick getaway.'

'Of course.' With an imperious sweep of his arm the young paediatrician held the media pack at bay. 'Mr Kingsley-Laird has another important engagement,' he told them. 'But our publicity officer will be happy to answer your questions.' To Jack, he murmured, 'Follow me.'

Once clear of the reception room, Jack thanked the doctor and made his excuses.

'There's someone in the children's ward I need to see.'

'Oh? You have a special interest in that ward?' the doctor asked hopefully, as if he sensed another donation in the wind.

'Ah—not especially. I was impressed by— by the—er—bright artwork.' With a brief saluting wave Jack turned quickly away.

His stomach was churning by the time he stepped through the doorway of the children's ward. He scanned the bright airy room, searching for Isabella, but all he could see were beds holding small children with an assortment of limbs in plaster.

Where in blue blazes was Isabella?

'Excuse me,' he called, hurrying towards a nurse. 'Can you tell me where I can find the volunteer who was working here in this ward an hour ago?'

'Do you mean Isabella?'

'Yes.'

'Oh, I'm afraid she's just left. I think she's gone home.'

Suppressing a curse, Jack resurrected his most charming smile. 'You don't happen to know where she lives, do you?'

The nurse's eyes narrowed as she studied him. 'We can't give out that kind of information.'

'No, I don't suppose you can,' he agreed, in his most conciliatory tone. But his hopes rose when he noted a telling gleam of suspicion in the nurse's eyes. Chances were she knew Isabella quite well. He glanced at her name badge. 'This is an emergency, Nancy. I have to see Isabella.'

Nurse Nancy made a business of sorting the array of medicine bottles on the tray in front of her.

'When will she be working here again?' Jack persisted.

'I'm not sure,' she said, keeping her eyes downcast as she studied a medicine label with exaggerated care.

An impatient, despairing tremor vibrated through him. So near and yet so far! Shoving his hands deep in his pockets, he squared his shoulders and leaned closer. 'What if I was to explain to you exactly *why* I must see this woman?'

Isabella was going to a party. Her first ordinary party as an ordinary girl. Like millions of single girls all over the world, she was getting ready to go out on a Saturday night.

It was just one of a host of new experiences she'd enjoyed recently. The first and most gratifying had been winning her father's approval to leave Amoria and come to Perth. But there'd been many more—finding her sweet little cottage, shopping for groceries in a supermarket, learning to cook, to grow potted herbs, to keep house. It was all such fun.

Now, fresh from her bath and wrapped in a red silk kimono, she smiled as she surveyed the things she'd bought for the party. In the little shop around the corner she'd found the perfect dress—soft and floaty, with copper-coloured flowers and shimmering mossy leaves on a black background.

And she'd found very sexy high-heeled, backless sandals—*kitten heels*, the girl in the shop had called them—and new sexy black underwear, a cheeky little beaded handbag with a parrot on the clasp, and new make-up— brighter than what she'd worn back home.

Very soon she would be heading off to a suburban flat brimming with fun-loving nurses and spunky young doctors.

And any minute now she would start to feel excited.

It was disappointing not to be excited yet, but she was blaming the weather. During the afternoon a storm had broken over Perth, and it had been raining heavily ever since. The darkness and dampness must have dulled her mood.

The sizzle in the stomach would come when she arrived at the party. Everything would be fine as long as she didn't think about Jack. Tonight she couldn't, wouldn't, *mustn't* think about him. This was the first night of her new, exciting, Post-Jack social life.

Parting the curtains on her bedroom window, she peered out at the rainy night and wondered for the hundredth time about the gypsy woman's prophecy. It was pathetically romantic of her to keep hoping that she might find lasting happiness in this country. She had to stop imagining that she might at any moment run into Jack.

But it was so hard—especially now that she'd seen the story on the early evening news. To think he'd been at the Royal Perth Hospital this morning.

This morning. If only she'd known she might have seen him. Spoken to him.

Stop it, she reprimanded herself. *Stop thinking about him. You'll ruin a perfectly good night. Jack's getting on with his life and you've got to try to get on with yours.*

She glanced back to the little travelling clock beside her bed and decided it was time to get dressed. Closing the curtain, she slipped out of her kimono and crossed to the bed. She'd put on her underwear first, then do her make-up before she put the dress on.

No doubt the sizzle would start once she was dressed and ready. She scooped up the black silk G-string panties, and at precisely the same moment her front doorbell rang.

Startled, she checked the time again. It had to be Nancy, calling to take her to the party, but she was terribly early. Heavens, now she would have to rush her preparations. And where should she ask Nancy to wait? Should she offer her a drink?

Feeling just a little fretful, Isabella reached for her kimono and tugged it around her again as she hurried in bare feet to answer the door.

There was a switch for the porch light in the hallway, and as she turned it on she saw the blurred outline of her caller and the black shape of an umbrella through the panel of amber glass in her door.

Unexpectedly, her stomach tightened.

Was this the beginning of the excitement she had hoped for?

'I'm afraid I'm not ready,' she called as she opened the door. And her heart stalled.

It wasn't Nancy.

Her knees gave way and she sagged against the doorjamb.

Jack!

The porch light splashed over him, highlighting the gilded tips of his brown hair, the craggy planes of his forehead, nose and cheekbones—the intense blue light in his eyes.

He'd propped his dripping umbrella against the wall of her porch, and now he stood with one hand behind his back. Drops of rain glistened on the shoulders of his dark jacket and rain splashes darkened the bottoms of his stone-coloured trousers. Beneath his jacket he wore a blue shirt that matched his eyes. The top buttons of the shirt were open and she saw dark, curling hair.

Jack. In the flesh.

'Hello, Isabella.'

She hardly heard his greeting above the savage thundering of her heartbeats. When she tried to reply her voice wouldn't work.

So many times in her dreams she'd experienced a moment like this. Jack striding back into her life. But the dreams had always turned to nightmares. Whenever Jack had come close enough for her to touch him he'd fractured into a thousand pieces.

She half expected it to happen now. If she blinked he might dissolve into raindrops and form a puddle at her feet.

'What are you doing here?' she managed to ask at last.

'I heard you were in town,' he said easily, as if they were no more than casual schoolfriends catching up on gossip.

'But how did you know I was here?'

'I saw you at the hospital this morning.'

'Really?'

'Then you performed a vanishing act—so I made a few discreet enquiries.' His mouth tilted into a faint smile, but his blue eyes remained intense and watchful. 'How are you, Carmen?'

'I'm—I'm very well, thank you, Jack.'

A gust of wind sent the rain slanting onto the porch, adding to the splashes on his trousers. 'Are you going to invite me inside?' he asked.

'I'm—I'm expecting someone at any moment,' she said, gripping the doorknob for support. 'I'm getting ready to go out.' Nervously she slid her hand over her hip and down her thigh.

His eyes shimmered as he watched the path her hand took, and then he let his gaze travel slowly over her. She felt absurdly self-conscious and exposed as she stood there in her bare feet and silky kimono, but she resisted an urge to yank the garment more tightly closed over her chest.

Jack released a deep breath and took a step closer. 'I need to talk to you, Isabella.'

'Why?' she whispered, pressing herself away from him and against the door as pulsing, scary excitement flashed through her.

In the dark, rainy street behind him tyres swished and splashed through a puddle. Car lights swept past, shining fuzzy and golden through the needles of rain. He glanced at the lights, then back to her. 'Do you remember a rainy night when you were beating at my door and I let you in?'

Oh, heavens! She'd been trying so hard not to think about that. Not the flooded creek, the storm, the dark bush. The lightning flashes. Not Jack in his hut...removing leeches, making her tea, giving up his bed for her. Or what had followed—on the river, in the tent...

'Isabella, would it help if I told you that your friend Nancy gave me her blessing to come here?'

Nancy? She felt dizzy and confused, as if she'd woken in the middle of a crazy, mixed-up dream. 'Perhaps Nancy knows something that I don't.'

From behind his back Jack produced a single long-stemmed dark red rose. She pressed her hands against her thumping heart and stared at him, and then at the raindrops glistening on the velvety folds of the rose petals, at the ivory silk ribbons fluttering from its thorny stem.

'I almost brought you Australian wildflowers, but decided to stick with tradition,' he said. Casting another glance out to the rain, then back to her, he shrugged shyly. 'I've come to ask you for a second chance.'

Her heart felt as if it had taken off down a ski slope. 'I don't understand,' she whispered, but they both knew she was lying.

In an exaggerated gesture Jack held the rose against his heart. 'Isabella, unless you want the entire street to watch me propose to you I think you should invite me inside.'

Before she could answer, he was propelling her into the house and pulling the door shut behind them. Her legs were shaking so badly she had to lean against the wall. She was trembling from the riot of emotions that filled her. She couldn't take her eyes off Jack. He looked so gorgeous.

Without any hesitation he walked into her little sitting room. In a daze, she followed, and wondered rather irrelevantly whether he liked the country farmhouse furniture she'd chosen.

'Please take a seat,' she said.

'I'd rather not.' He set the rose down on the coffee table, and when he straightened he stood very still, looking at her. His throat worked. 'I'm afraid I'm rather nervous.'

'That makes two of us,' she whispered. Outside in the dark, beyond her new floral curtains, the rain lashed against the windowpane. 'But if it helps I'd very much like to hear what you have to say, Jack.'

His mouth twitched as if he'd tried to smile but no smile had arrived. Then he plunged his hands deeply into his trouser pockets. The movement nudged his jacket wide open, and she couldn't help admiring the very masculine way his blue shirt tapered from his broad shoulders and chest to the trimness of his waist and hips.

'The thing is,' he said, 'I made a hopeless hash of asking you to marry me when I was in Amoria. You were in a state of shock and I went at things like a bull at a gate. I think I know why you rejected me, and I don't blame you, so I've come to ask if I can try again.'

Tears filled her eyes and a tremor shook her smile. 'Why should people only have one chance?' *But, please, if you don't tell me you love me this time I think I might die.*

He smiled nervously and his eyes shimmered. 'I love you, Isabella.'

'Oh, Jack.' Her heart swelled with a painful, uplift of longing. 'Are you quite sure?'

He stared at her in amazement. 'I'm absolutely sure. I'm more than sure. I'm desperately, madly in love with you. You've got to believe me.'

'It's just that at Killymoon you were so certain we had no future. After your wife—'

He gave an impatient shake of his head. 'I was fooling myself. I had the cracked idea that I could avoid more pain by keeping you at bay. I was crazy, because it was already too late.' He stepped closer. 'Damn fool that I was, I didn't realise that I was already in love with you.' He reached for her hands, gripped them in his. 'These past months have been hell. I can only be happy with you. I want to devote the rest of my life to making you happy.'

Jack loved her. She could hear it in his words and in the choke in his voice, and she could see it in the sheen in his eyes, feel it in the tremble in his hands.

'I'm so sorry I sent you away,' she said. 'I've been desperately miserable too. But, you see, I thought you'd been forced into proposing by my father. You didn't say anything about loving me.'

'I know, I know. I can't believe I was so stupid.'

'And I needed you to love me as much as I love you.'

'Oh, Isabella.' With a tortured groan he hauled her into his arms. He held her against his thudding heart, embracing her fiercely, as if he feared she might vanish. He buried his face in her hair. 'I love you, my dear girl. I love you. I love you.' Tucking her head against his shoulder, he pressed his lips to her forehead. 'You *must* believe me.'

'I believe you.'

'I've even found out how to say I love you in French.'

'Tell me.'

'*Je t'aime.*'

'Oh, darling Jack.' She was smiling and crying at once, laughing through her tears. *'Je t'aime.'* She kissed the gorgeous underside of his jaw. *'Je t'aime. Je t'adore.'*

Jack kissed her earlobe. 'And that's not all. I can also say it in Spanish.' He grinned and kissed her other ear. *'Te amo.'*

'Te amo,' she whispered happily, kissing his neck.

He kissed her eyelids. *'Je t'aime.'* He kissed her throat. *'Te amo.'* He kissed her chin. 'I'd better warn you, I'm going to learn how to say I love you in every language.'

'Don't make me cry,' she sobbed joyfully, turning her face to capture his next kiss. And at last he was kissing her mouth. She met him with eager, hungry, open lips. And he returned her kiss deeply. Taking her. Claiming her as she longed to be claimed. She was *his*.

Jack's woman.

His hands cradled her head and his kiss was hot and wonderfully fierce. Possessive. Hungry. Isabella clung to him, stunned by the jolt of violent happiness that surged through her. Jack, her gorgeous, gorgeous Jack, wanted her. Loved her. *Loved her!*

She let her head fall back so that their kiss could deepen. His hands travelled over her shoulders, moulding and exploring their shape, then slid down her arms. Up again, more slowly. Building her fever.

Oh, she loved his hands. Loved the way he touched her. She'd been too long apart from him. This was where she and Jack belonged— touching, loving. When his hand reached her breast a pleasure bomb seemed to explode inside her. She tugged impatiently at the ties of her kimono, letting it fall open, wanting no barrier between her skin and his touch.

Jack groaned, and she felt a tremor run through him as he touched her bare skin. 'Isabella…'

'I love you. *Je t'adore.*'

His hands spanned her ribs and he scattered a sweet, swift trail of kisses over her bare shoulder, then moved lower.

Oh, yes. Her breath escaped in a throaty moan. She needed his mouth on her skin more than her next heartbeat.

A loud ringing sounded on the front door.

Isabella froze, momentarily puzzled. And then remembered. 'Oh, goodness, will that be Nancy?' she whispered.

Holding her close, Jack half turned towards the hallway. 'No doubt she wants to make sure I haven't botched my second chance.'

'Oh, dear.'

'What do you mean by that—oh, dear?'

'Well…actually…you *have* botched it.'

Jack blinked. 'Pardon?'

'As far as I know, you haven't actually asked me to marry you yet.'

'You will, though, won't you?'

'Sure thing, mate.'

He looked down at her with a quizzical smile.

The doorbell rang again, more insistently, but Isabella ignored it as she wound her arms around Jack's neck. 'That's Australian for, Yes, my darling Jack, there's nothing in this world I want more than to be your wife.'

His blue eyes sparkled as he dropped another kiss on her shoulder. With an exaggerated sigh he pulled her clothing demurely into place and retied the belt. 'I guess we'd better go tell Nancy the good news.'

'Too bad I'll be missing that party.'

'But I'm planning one of our own.'

'Oh, yes. Let's hurry.'

EPILOGUE

IT WAS a perfect moonlit night. No clouds. Just the velvet-black sky stretched in a high arc to provide a stark backdrop for the silver half-moon and the brilliant sweep of stars.

Isabella and Jack spread a rug on the lake's shore and lay on their backs, gazing up at the heavens while close by in the hut their daughter Annie lay snugly asleep in her little cot.

'Do the individual stars of the Southern Cross have names?' Isabella asked.

'Sure.' Jack leaned on one elbow and raised his other arm to point. 'You start with Alpha, there, and then there's Beta, Gamma, Delta, and the tiny one in between them is Epsilon.'

'Mmmm…Alpha,' she repeated, and shot him a slow, cheeky smile. 'Perhaps we could call our next baby Alpha?'

'You're joking?'

She gave him a playful poke in the ribs. 'Don't you think Alpha has a certain panache? Annie and Alpha. Or perhaps you'd prefer Epsilon?'

Jack chuckled and reached under her T-shirt to caress the gentle bump of her stomach where their second child lay. He felt so much more relaxed this time round. When Annie had been born he'd been a bundle of nerves, ter- rified for Isabella and for the child. Terrified for himself—that he might lose them.

But Isabella, bless her, had been serene and calm. 'Everything will be fine,' she'd reas- sured him.

And it had been. They'd flown to Amoria for the confinement, and Isabella had chosen a water birth at an exclusive hospital in Valdenza. In a dark room lit only by candle- light their daughter had arrived with a mini- mum of fuss or distraction.

Such a sweet little dark-haired angel.

He'd been filled with awe when he held her for the first time. He'd cradled her sturdy, still damp little body, felt her tiny, vigorous movements, and had been completely disarmed when she'd opened her mouth and tried to nuzzle him.

'She's hungry already,' he'd whispered in amazement. She'd been so healthy, so full of life.

And Isabella had been positively glowing with health and happiness.

'Would you like to call her Annie, after your first baby?' she'd asked.

And he'd wept. Tears of sorrow for his fragile, red-haired Annie, and joy for this beautiful, robust daughter with raven curls like her mother's. He hadn't been able to thank Isabella then, but he'd done so a hundred times since.

Now, as they watched the stars, Isabella snuggled closer against his shoulder and the night wrapped around them like a warm, silent cocoon. 'Aren't you glad I persuaded you to come here to Pelican's End for our wedding anniversary?' she asked.

'Very,' he murmured, kissing her. 'But, sweet girl, anywhere with you seems perfect.' He traced the soft curve of her cheek with his hand and watched the moonlight silver her lovely profile. 'Valdenza, Killymoon, Perth— as long as you're there, I'm a happy man.'

He hadn't known it was possible to find such peace in his life. The past three years had brought the private joy of his marriage, the happy merger of his company with his parents' business, and the success of Isabella's plan to use her royal allowance to launch the Christos Tenni Institute for Research.

'You know I love you to bits,' he said. 'Especially this bit.' He trailed his mouth over her lips, already parted in a warm, soft invitation.

'*Nagligivaget,*' he murmured, pulling her more closely against him.

'*Naglig*—what?'

'*Nagligivaget.*'

'What's that?'

'It's Inuit for I love you.'

'Oh, you darling man. How many languages are you up to now?'

'I've lost count.'

'You're so special, Jack,' she whispered, and, looking up at the Southern Cross again she smiled. '*Je t'aime.*'

He kissed her tenderly. '*Te amo*, Carmen.'

MILLS & BOON® PUBLISH EIGHT LARGE PRINT TITLES A MONTH. THESE ARE THE EIGHT TITLES FOR AUGUST 2004

---❦---

THE MISTRESS PURCHASE
Penny Jordan

THE OUTBACK MARRIAGE RANSOM
Emma Darcy

A SPANISH MARRIAGE
Diana Hamilton

HIS VIRGIN SECRETARY
Cathy Williams

THE DUKE'S PROPOSAL
Sophie Weston

PRINCESS IN THE OUTBACK
Barbara Hannay

MARRIAGE IN NAME ONLY
Barbara McMahon

A PROFESSIONAL ENGAGEMENT
Darcy Maguire

MILLS & BOON®

Live the emotion

0704 Ro